States. As we docked into New York harbour, we were obliged to register ourselves. "This is finally the moment, little Rebecca robin, to begin anew," he whispered to me. So that girl, Rebecca Mortkowicz, the girl I was when you knew me, no longer exists. Papa and I left a large part of our Polish selves behind us, shards along the trail... And it is better so, but you will read all about it in the pages that follow.

Diary of Rebecca Mortkowicz

13 April 1938

Before I start to write this diary in earnest – well, it is to be a journal as much as a diary, jottings, thoughts, scribbles... Anything I like, in fact, but especially the words and thoughts will be companions to me, a listening ear, when I will be far away from all my friends – I want to jot down a few details about myself, about how and why my parents and I have found ourselves in this scary situation. I want to write a little about myself and my family, in case anything else even more terrible happens to us. In case all that remains of me are these few pages, I hope that someone, somewhere, will find this book and that our story will be recorded.

My name is Rebecca Mortkowicz. I am Polish, born on 10th May 1927 close to the centre of Warsaw (the capital of Poland) at number 40, Zlota Street. It is really a pretty area of the city where we live. There are lots of flowers and, although quite poor in parts, it is very clean and well-maintained and there are many other Jewish families like ourselves who live close by us.

It is mid-April and the snows have melted from the streets. The cobbled lanes and squares of the old town of

Warsaw – in Polish we call the old town *Stare Miasto* – with its tall, coloured houses, seemed jolly and a happy place to be. Until yesterday afternoon.

I was in an excellent mood yesterday afternoon, strolling, skipping through the streets, hurrying past the factory district and streets of tenements. I had come top of my class in a maths exam, and I hate maths so it felt like a real triumph. As I reached our quarter of the city, I noticed the very tiniest buds appearing on the trees and that made me even more exuberant because summer is on the way. The winters here can be long and very bleak, and we always look forward to the arrival of warmer days and natural colours.

When I shoved open the door from school, yelling "hello", bursting to tell Mama about my triumphant test result, I discovered that my father was there. This was a surprise because he normally works at the hospital till quite late. He was standing alongside my mother and was looking so very grave as he held out his hand to draw me close to him. My immediate thought was that he had received some very bad news.

"I have something to say to you, my little Rebecca robin. Something not so easy to hear and you will need to be very brave."

"What is it?" I muttered, looking from one to the other. I could see then that my mother, who is always tired from long sleepless nights looking after my little brother, Marek, had been crying. Father cleared his throat and slowly broke his news to me. I was completely shocked and because of all that was revealed, I never found the opportunity to tell them how well I had done at school.

"You must pack your belongings, my Rebecca, and prepare to leave this home of ours."

I was horrified and scared. Were my parents about to throw me out of the house? No, that was not the situation, but the reality was equally frightening. And what is more, Father warned me very seriously that every detail he was about to confide was to be kept a very secure secret. My legs were trembling as he sat down and lifted me onto his knees and told me what was soon to happen...

There is a man called Adolf Hitler who is trying to gain control of our country. Hitler, who has been ruling our neighbouring country of Germany since 1933, seems to be a horrid evil human being, judging by what father told me yesterday evening, who wants to be in charge of everywhere. In the beginning, I was too small to know anything about such political problems, but my father, whose name is Otto Mortkowicz, and who is a very educated man, a physician and paediatrician (a children's doctor), who speaks several languages and has contacts all across Europe, has been keeping in touch with everything that is happening outside Poland. Father has friends living abroad who have alerted him to the possible dangers that might lie ahead. My father, I call him *Tata*, which is Polish for Daddy, has no desire to leave our home, particularly because on 26th July 1936 my mother, who I nicknamed *Matkować*, gave birth to my baby brother, Marek.

However, it is becoming clear that this ruler of Germany, Adolf Hitler, is determined to conquer Poland. His most likely strategy will be to invade our land. It is for this reason my father has decided *we must leave*.

"But what about everyone else living in Poland?" I cried. "We cannot be the only family in danger."

"The Jewish citizens are the ones at greatest risk," *Tata* explained. "Even those of us who are not orthodox. Please don't fret, I have organized a comfortable and dependable place for us, a temporary home, until it is safe to return. I hope it will not be for more than a few months."

"But where, *Tata*? Is it far?"

"I will tell you soon, but not just yet."

I never argue with *Tata* but none of this makes any sense. I want to run away, to hide until he changes his mind, until everything is back to normal. Where can this "temporary home" be?

So, in spite of my small success at school, yesterday turned out to be a horrid day.

21 April 1938

I will be celebrating my eleventh birthday in just a few weeks, but Marek is still a baby. He is barely able to toddle. Father said this evening that he considers it too risky to take Marek along with us on this journey we are soon to embark upon, and so my brother is to be left behind with my mother's unmarried younger sister, Aunt Irina, who lives with us.

"But when will we see them again," I protested, "and where are we going?"

"We are going to Paris, to my brother, your uncle Adam, and his wife, Lidia. As soon as we can, Rebecca, just as soon as we have set up home in France, we will send for Marek and Irina. Tomorrow, you and your mother are to go into the city to buy yourselves sturdy walking boots and some travelling clothes. You are not to mention anything of this at school, is that understood?"

I nodded, feeling the fear of uncertainty return.

"Now, you must think about what you need to take with you. Choose carefully. Take only what you can carry and what you cannot do without."

But I didn't want to think about it at all. I don't want to

go. I am happy in Warsaw. I am doing well at school and I like my friends. I don't understand why we must leave, particularly just before my birthday, while the rest of my friends can stay. Father's answer to this was that it is more difficult for Jewish people. "Hitler does not like our sort."

But many of my friends are also Jewish. If they stay behind and it is not safe, what will happen to them? If it is going to be dangerous for them here, why can't I warn them? Surely, that would be a fair thing to do? Why can't they come with us?

I feel very confused.

28th April 1938

It is evening and I am exhausted.

My mother, father and I left the city of Warsaw at dawn in a meat-delivery truck, which smelt horrid, driven by a man Father is acquainted with and who he had engaged for the task. *Tata* had treated the man's son when he was suffering from pneumonia and judged the tradesman to be an honourable and honest sort who knew better than to gossip. *Tata* was concerned that our luggage might raise interest from neighbours or that we might be stopped and questioned if we left by the central railway station in

Jerozolimskie Street. Although it is not illegal for Jews to travel, *Tata* still insisted on discretion. The most important reason for his secrecy is because we are leaving Marek and Aunt Irina behind. He wants no problems for them and the fewer people who know of our escape, the better. It is essential they are safe, he said.

But surely everyone is going to know something is wrong when I don't turn up for school tomorrow, or the next day and the day after that…?

Our travels this morning led us west and out of the city. I turned my head and peered hard through the truck window, back across the winding Vistula river, flanked by trees with freshly shooting leaves, to a place that I could no longer see: the pink house that has been our home all my life. My baby brother was sleeping when we left. I stroked his fat cheeks, wiped the dribble from his lips while silently asking myself when will we all be together again. I have no idea what lies ahead. None of us do.

Once clear of danger and out in the countryside, we drove for over an hour before entering a village. It seemed very silent with not too many inhabitants about other than those we had seen working in the fields. Our driver pulled up outside an isolated farmhouse and we, with our cases, piled out. We left the truck to return to Warsaw while a ruddy-faced farmer's wife, who had been expecting us, welcomed us into her house. There we sat on a wooden bench in silence for ages until the woman offered us a bowl to wash ourselves. When her husband, the farmer, and their two tall sons, all three with worn hands and cracked nails, finally arrived, we ate together in their cramped kitchen. Hardly a word was spoken. Meal over, we were led out by candlelight to a barn where we passed the night on a bed of straw. I could not sleep and I am sure that I heard Mother close by, softly sobbing.

29 April 1938

We rose before daybreak. My back was aching and I was tired. Then, travelling upright like a gaggle of land labourers in the farmer's wooden hay cart, we were ferried, horse-drawn, to a remote town and dropped off in front of a small country railway station. We said our brief farewells and gave thanks to the farmer and then we boarded a steam train. The station master with his bulbous nose and great walrus moustache blew his whistle and the train lurched forward, chugging us onwards towards the Polish border. The views through the windows, looking out at the countryside and the silent farmlands, were very beautiful and the sun was shining softly, though it was not very warm. "This is my homeland," I kept repeating to myself. "I have never been this far from Warsaw before, have never set eyes on this lovely countryside and now I am leaving it."

I glanced across at my parents. They were both silent. Father was clutching a book he had been reading, but now his eyes were closed. Mother was fidgeting with a handkerchief, staring at her gloved hands. I thought I would burst into tears…

I must stop. I will write again tomorrow or the next day, recounting more about our dangerous travels. I am too exhausted now and must sleep. We need all our strength to keep going.

2 May 1938

Continuing the story of our escape…

Once we arrived at the final station, we disembarked and gathered up our luggage. It was then I understood why *Tata* had been so strict about what we were allowed to bring with us. We began to walk with our individual loads, doubling-back on ourselves, trekking away from the frontier line. Father pulled out a sheet of paper with a roughly sketched map on it and we made our way to a clearing in a wood, marked on his paper with a big black X. There we waited until after dark. The farmer's wife had given us a package containing fresh milk, cheese, bread and three thick slices of fresh juicy ham. We are Jews and pig meat is forbidden to us. We are not at all a strictly orthodox family, but all the same, we left the meat in its cloth wrapping. The rest of our picnic tasted delicious and I ate ravenously but mother barely touched a mouthful.

"Eat," commanded *Tata*, "you'll need all your strength, Ruby." But she shook her head.

Father had arranged for two contacts, friends of friends, from Berlin, members of a Jewish support committee, to meet us at the precise point where we were hiding, just east of the border. When they arrived – both quite young with beards; one with glasses – they furnished us with three sets of false identity papers, talked at length to my father in German about matters I could not understand, and then when the moment was right, signalled us to follow. Before setting off, Father explained to Mother and me that the border was controlled by armed soldiers who would shoot us if they spotted us, that the frontier zones were secured and closed off with barbed wire and in some areas even landmines. Also, there were German patrol tanks, which we would have to avoid at all costs. Our guides knew the best route and the exact moment to get us through safely, but we were to keep together and never lose sight of one another. I felt really scared when I heard all this.

The two men led us on foot into Germany well after dark, crossing the frontier through a sweet-smelling forest. I remember so clearly the sounds of that night – a stream's fast flow somewhere distant, an owl's weird screeching (it was really spooky), the putting of a patrol tank engine, and the anxious silence between us. We had been instructed to be as quiet as possible and not speak at all.

As day broke, the two men wished us well and then hurried away. We were exhausted. I could hear a dog barking in the distance and it made me feel even more scared, much more than the owl's call. I have never been afraid of dogs or any animal for that matter, but that morning, smelling the pine needles on the ground underfoot, my stomach rumbling loudly from hunger, I was scared in a way that made me shiver from head to foot. I was standing on foreign soil for the first time in my life and I suddenly knew that the journey we had taken so far and the journey that lay ahead of us was no ordinary adventure. I understood the importance of the months of planning my father had put into all of this. We were leaving our lives behind us. Our family had been divided into two. I wrapped my arms tight around my mother, dear *Matkować*, who though not ill was grieving the separation from my baby brother and my aunt, her sister.

3 May 1938

Our false documents are enabling us to cross Germany without suspicion. Mine is in the name of Anneliese Meler. Does she really exist? I keep asking myself. We are the Meler family.

7 May 1938

We are crossing from east to west, some distance south of the city of Berlin through a region called Brandenburg. We are attempting at all times to avoid the big cities where Father fears we are more likely to be stopped and investigated. Most nights we sleep under the stars or creep into a farmer's barn, making sure we are on our way before daybreak, before anyone finds us. Slowly, we are making our way towards Frankfurt, miles and miles across Germany.

10 May 1938

We are somewhere along the road. I don't know where, but still walking, walking, walking. Sometimes we take a bus through a town or trek through a forest. Twice we have ridden on trains but that is riskier. We buy food in small grocery stores in little towns, places where we are less likely to be looked at with suspicion, or if there is anything edible at the roadsides, we help ourselves, but it is too early in the season for fruit. Father does the shopping because he speaks the language. Mother and I keep out of sight. We have been living on bread and cheese mostly. *Tata* and I have eaten cooked sausage meat but mother refuses to. We buy milk from farmers. I long for a hot meal and my bed. Today is my tenth birthday. I am too tired and sad to even think about it, or about all that we have left behind us.

27 May 1938

Finally, onwards, chugging along on a local train to Germany's western border town of Trier, neighbouring the State of Luxembourg.

9 June 1938

We have been wearing our feet out, walking through the night, walking through the days. How I hate these boots! Walking slowly some days because Mama is becoming tired. Occasionally we have managed to beg lifts in a horse-drawn cart and once in a large truck transporting cheeses. The driver was kind and gave us a creamy round sample to take with us on our way. After almost two weeks we have crossed the width of Luxembourg and reached the French border. Tomorrow, France. What a relief! Journey's end is in sight.

10 June 1938

Horrid luck today!

We have no visas, no *permis de séjour*, and the French official has refused to give us entry visas. My father argued, almost begged with him this morning, but still he shook his head. The official glanced at us – we must look like a family of tramps! – then once again at our false German papers. He shook his head and sent us back into Luxembourg.

"You are unable to enter France without the correct papers. There is nothing I can do for you," he concluded gruffly.

13 June 1938

We are all in a state of desperation and downheartedness. We have spent the last three days in a rather expensive guesthouse. They call it an *auberge*. We are trying to sort out a solution to our problem, but so far nothing. Has all this travelling and trekking been for nothing? Mother just lies on her bed, sleeping or staring at the ceiling. She seems to have no will for anything. I think she is missing Marek badly, but she doesn't say so. I am missing him too and all my friends. While we were on the move there was no real time to think, but now, cooped up inside this funny little hotel, all my fears come rushing at me. What is to become of us? Surely, it would be better if we just turned round and went back home?

15 June 1938

Father has located a professional guide. They are known as *passeurs*, smugglers. For a handsome sum, he is going to accompany us by foot and lead us clandestinely into northern France. We will be entering the country illegally because we have no papers, no resident or tourist permits, not even false papers like those we used in Germany. It is a huge risk, but what choice do we have? If we are caught we will be thrown out of France and either sent back to Poland or kept in a place where other escaped Polish families are also being detained.

Mother said today that she wants to return home. She and *Tata* have been arguing, in hushed voices, thinking I don't hear them. They don't ask me my opinion, but now that we have someone to guide us, I believe we should keep going. We have come too far to give up now. There is no turning back, and once we are safe in France, Marek and Aunt Irina can join us.

20 June 1938

We are in France! Yes, we made it. My heart nearly stopped when we heard a shot ring out close by us in the night, but it was only a man out hunting. He must have been a poacher trying to catch himself some rabbits. I wish he'd given us one. We are so in need of lashings of hot food. I am longing for a huge plate of fish with raisin sauce made the way Mama makes it. And cabbage leaves stuffed with rice, and bagels with sour cream or curd cheese and onions, sorrel soup… I must stop or I will DIE of hunger. I dream about food all the time.

I haven't been able to keep up my diary. I lost or forgot my pencil-case somewhere along the road. It is late June, I think. I cannot pinpoint the precise date. I am beginning to lose track of time. Also, we frequently sleep by day and travel by night and everything becomes confusing. Mid-summer is approaching. Of that I am sure because I have always been fond of nature, and I have been studying the flowers and shrubs growing around us. It's easy when you live out of doors! The days are getting hotter and our bags heavier.

We have been hiding in an area known as the Moselle region. It is really pretty with lots of vineyards and tall trees. The fields smell sweet. We helped ourselves to bunches of grapes off the vines, but they were unripe and rather too sour.

Tonight, we arrived at a big town, Nancy (where I bought a box of pencils). If all goes well and we are not arrested for having no papers, we are intending to take a train to Paris tomorrow. We have found a tiny guesthouse in the city for tonight; one small room between us because our funds are growing limited, but at least we have water for washing and will be given a warm meal.

2 July 1938

Hooray! Our train drew into Paris yesterday, arriving at a huge railway station, the Gare de l'Est, where we were met by my father's older brother, Adam, and his wife, Lidia. He so tall; she so short and round and decorated with long pearl necklaces. They greeted us warmly and took us immediately to their house where they gave us two rooms,

24

"A safe harbour", said Uncle Adam, until we can organize a better living situation for ourselves. My uncle Adam, whom I had never set eyes on before, is very nice. I really like him. He has a twinkling smile and he winks at me so that I won't be shy. Lidia dished up a groaning great meal, even better than I have been dreaming about: onion soup with slices of toast floating in it and strips of melty cheese sinking in it followed by stewed lamb and potatoes. It was delicious. Diary written and now bed. Tonight I will be sleeping in a room of my own with a small desk, a big comfortable bed with clean sheets, and what a treat to unpack my bag and hang up my very scruffy-looking clothes.

4 July 1938

Paris! Ooh la la!

The five of us went for a long walk this morning down by the River Seine where we saw people working on barges moored at the water's edge. The boats are homes as well as the means for livelihoods. From there we went to Avenue George V, which is very posh with grand carriages descending and ascending it. After, we turned right, into the Champs Elysées. It was all so thrilling. Paris is so beautiful and the people in the streets all look so well-dressed (not those on the riverboats). Uncle Adam and Lidia, who is rather quiet and very pale-skinned, like Mama, live on the right bank of the Seine. The river divides the city into two, snaking right through the heart of Paris, and many boats travel up and down it. Their house is very tall with five storeys. I think they must be very rich. The rooms are high-ceilinged and spacious with shiny wooden floors that squeak when you walk on them. Everywhere smells of beeswax. The rooms are sumptuous with heavy, sweeping curtains and furniture of polished wood: chairs, tables, sideboards, dressers, wardrobes with great big metal keys in the doors and, dotted all over the place, are displays of porcelain figurines. I am not allowed to touch one single thing in case I break something. From the two upper floors, and that includes my slope-ceiling attic room way at the top of the house, you can see right across the river to the Eiffel Tower. If I stand on tiptoe and look out of the window, I can see all the boats moving up and down the river.

I am longing to start exploring the city by myself.

5 July 1938

Uncle Adam emigrated to France in 1922, after a war. He and *Tata* refer to it as the Great War. My uncle has been living and working here very successfully as a psychiatrist ever since. He met Lidia here. She is not Jewish, nor a psychiatrist, nor Polish. She is a music teacher, I think. She definitely has a job because she mentioned it at dinner. Not like Mama who has always stayed home to look after me and Marek and keep the house.

They have no children. I wonder why. Perhaps they prefer to have a house full of rare and fragile objects that no one is allowed to touch.

6 July 1938

Aunt Lidia was playing a beautiful song on her phonograph in the drawing room this afternoon. *"Le Chaland Qui Passe"*. I asked her what the title means. *"The Barge That Passes By"*.

Like all those working their way up and down the river, I exclaimed. Yes. After she translated all the words for me, she said I must learn French. She has offered to give me lessons. One class every evening. We start tomorrow. I cannot go to school without it, she says. Both she and my uncle are being very kind to us. Father says they are taking a big risk hiding an entire family of illegal immigrants.

"Illegal immigrants, is that what we are?" I asked him.

"Well, yes, we are stateless," he replied.

It sounds worrying.

An entire family? No, we are half a family...

26 July 1938

Marek is two today... Both my parents were very quiet and I did not remind them of the day. They surely know it themselves.

17 August 1938

Having no home of our own in Paris is sometimes a bit awkward, but we are living in our own two rooms and they are light and airy. I have my own space and all is well, and I love listening to Lidia's music as the notes weave their way up the winding stairs and out through the open windows. But Mama is not so happy. She really misses housekeeping and cooking and running her own home. Here, Aunt Lidia insists on taking charge of everything herself. There is a maid who comes in every morning to clean while Lidia gives private music lessons. She teaches singing, piano and violin. How amazing.

These days are also very difficult for poor *Tata* because he cannot find work as a doctor. He is highly qualified, but he does not have the correct papers and we are illegal. He has managed to gain employment at a local food market, unloading boxes of vegetables and packed meat products but he is not making sufficient money to find us somewhere of our own to live, particularly because out of what we have, he puts a bit aside each week to send back to Warsaw, funds for Irina and Marek towards their expenses to come and join us.

Almost all our savings, the money *Tata* brought out of Poland, has been spent on getting us here, including a large sum to the *passeur* who accompanied us into France.

25 September 1938

I have had no time to write in my diary. Exhausted! I started school almost three weeks ago and in the evenings I have homework as well as my French lessons with Aunt Lidia. It's great being with kids my own age again. I love my parents, but I have been missing my friends badly. My school is in Montparnasse, quite a distance from here. There are others attending who are also from Jewish families, who have arrived from other countries, whose families have also escaped. Quite a few are from Germany. I spoke to a boy with wild red hair and spectacles wearing a big floppy grey cardigan. He is from Berlin. His name is Ludwig and his parents are trying to get him to England. They believe he will be "out of harm's way" there.

"But it's safe here, isn't it?" I asked him.

Ludwig just shrugged.

The teachers speak of the problems building in Europe. When I got home from school, I asked Uncle Adam what the problems building in Europe are. He explained that Hitler is obsessed with expanding his territory into a Greater Germany and for that he needs to conquer other countries. He predicts that Poland will soon come under Hitler's control. Uncle says Hitler wants more *Lebensraum*. I did not understand this word. It is German and means Living Space. Since we have walked miles and miles across Germany, I would say that Hitler has plenty of living space, and he is just being greedy!

Tonight is the eve of Rosh Hashanah, Erev Rosh Hashanah. Tomorrow is our Jewish new year. *Shana Tova!* Happy New Year! We all gathered together at Uncle Adam's big dining-room table and lit lots of candles and talked about Poland and what it was like when Father and Uncle Adam were growing up there. Lidia was born in Paris, she told us. She is a Roman Catholic and they have different holidays to celebrate.

27 September 1938

Father and Uncle Adam went to the synagogue this morning. They took Uncle's special prayer book. I have never seen one before. Aunt Lidia, of course, did not go and nor did Mama nor I. We are not a very religious family, but Father said he wanted to pray for peace and for our family. During our Rosh Hashanah meal tonight, my father mentioned that he dreams of taking us to America. The United States is where he sees our future, but not until we are reunited with Marek and Aunt Irina.

"Until we are together again, we will remain in Paris."

America, I cannot picture such an idea, and it is so far away.

We have no news from Aunt Irina yet. Today of all days, I had hoped we would hear from her.

We ate gefilte fish and then scrummy apples cooked in honey. Aunt Lidia let Mama prepare the baked apples. I don't think they really like each other, but as today is like a Judgement Day in our religion, I think they were making a special effort to be nice together. Maybe this is also why Mama is always sad. Maybe it's because Aunt Lidia is not Jewish and spends lots of time playing music. She has a grand piano. I would love to ask her to teach me to play, but she already gives up her time for my French lessons so I cannot be too demanding.

28 September 1938

Two girls from my class at school have not been seen for several days. A boy called Henri told me they have been sent to England. He said that his parents think that the sooner all Jews have gone from France, the easier it will be for everyone. I don't like him now for saying that.

1 October 1938

Hooray! *Tata* has started to practise privately as a family doctor and a paediatrician. He has two patients but is hoping to build up a good reputation so that people will bring their children to him for treatment, and then soon he will have many more patients. He is not working in a hospital, so it will be difficult because we have no home of our own where families can wait and no consulting rooms. Also, he will not be able to declare this work.

"I am optimistic though, my little robin," he told me. He

frequently calls me his "little robin", and I like it when he does. It makes me feel special.

5 October 1938

Yom Kippur. In our faith it is our Day of Atonement. We are not allowed to work or go to school or do anything. The thing I find most difficult is that we have to fast for 25 hours and it is the only part of our faith that my father is strict about. Otherwise, he is quite unorthodox and we are like everyone else.

29 October 1938

Father said at dinner last night that all Jews with Polish citizenship have been evicted from Germany. Imagine if we had still been there and our false papers had been discovered. An English politician, Winston Churchill, has declared that western Europe should be preparing itself for war against Hitler. I hope he is just trying to frighten Hitler.

12 November 1938

Kristallnacht. What is it? It means "Night of the Broken Glass" in German. Everyone is talking about it in hushed voices, and they seem very upset, but no one will explain it to me. I hate grown-up secrets but something very bad seems to have been happening.

13 November 1938

It was raining so heavily today. I cannot explain it but I felt frightened by the weather and the mood of everyone around me. What has happened, what is going on? Are we in danger?

14 November 1938

It seems that a Polish Jew, seventeen years old, shot a German diplomat in the German Embassy here in Paris seven days ago and since then there have been reprisals – reprisals are punishments – on Jews in Germany. A pogrom has begun. People are being hurt, arrested, thrown out of their homes.

Ludwig was not at school today, and when I asked another boy, Samuel, where he was, he whispered that Ludwig and his family have fled to England.

15 November 1938

A letter arrived for us from Warsaw. It was so good to hear from home.

Aunt Irina has written that she and Marek are well but that everybody in the city is becoming very nervous about Mr Hitler's behaviour. When she read the news, Mama became very angry with *Tata*. Why did we leave them behind? she cried. What was the sense of such a decision? I hate to see her in such a temper – it is very unlike her – and I hate to see how her words distress my father, but I have asked myself the same question. Why didn't we wait and leave Poland together as a family? This separation is hurting us all.

22 November 1938

Father has sent every last centime he has saved to my aunt so that she and Marek can make their escape as soon as possible. "Join us here in Paris as soon as you can," he wrote to Aunt Irina. I am not quite sure where we are all going to live, and I think *Tata* is concerned about that too, which, he says, was the reason he has been holding back. Uncle Adam is very calm about the problem. "You are not to worry about anything," he smiles. "Problems have a way of resolving themselves."

Aunt Lidia looks less assured. Even during our French lessons in the drawing room after school, she seems different; a bit withdrawn. Maybe she is worried. She was playing that Tino Rossi song again "*Le Chaland Qui Passe*". She told me it comes from a very wonderful film, *L'Atalante*. She was quite shocked when I told her that I have never seen a film, never been to a picture house.

"But there are picture houses in Warsaw, surely?" she cried.

Yes, there are, but I never visited any. My aunt shook her head in disbelief.

24 November 1938

Mama is happier than I have seen her since we left home. She talks non-stop of her sister's arrival and how different life will be when we are all together again and when we have found a little place to live. Two minutes later, she is dreaming of when we will all return together to Warsaw, of our little pink house at number 40, Zlota Street. Sometimes I think I have almost forgotten Zlota Street with all the flowers in the gardens, but I love to see Mama smiling. She looks so beautiful. She was even humming this evening in the kitchen as she chopped potatoes.

12 December 1938

Another letter arrived. Aunt Irina has not received any money yet. What can have happened? But the letter was quite out of date, more than two months old, so maybe by now she has received the first instalments of the payments.

23 December 1938

It is almost Christmas. All the French people are preparing to celebrate, living as though this will be their very last holiday. We have never observed these days. Christmas is a Christian event, but Uncle Adam and Lidia are planning on throwing a big party tomorrow evening. They have invited hundreds of people. It is good for business, it will help your father, Uncle Adam explained, while Aunt Lidia was very animated, buzzing to and fro with all the preparations.

All I care about is that we are still not together as a family.

25 December 1938

I am exhausted. It was a huge party. Everyone was drinking wine. Before supper while Aunt Lidia played the piano all the guests sat silently listening and then applauded. I felt quite envious of her skill. Father met loads of people working in the medical profession. Uncle Adam was pleased about the connections. So was *Tata*. Maybe it will help him find a proper job so that we can be legal and have our own home.

This morning, Aunt Lidia took me to a religious service at the Cathédrale Notre Dame de Paris. It was incredible. The church, with its immense, towering ceilings, with paintings and high walls with coloured glass windows, was packed. People were kneeling and standing and singing hymns and lining up to be blessed, or something. There were several priests who are like rabbis, only Catholic. It was all quite solemn and yet not unhappy. Today is the day Jesus Christ, their saviour, was born.

As we walked home through the cold sharp streets, feet echoing against cobbled stones, I asked Aunt Lidia if Christ was born in Paris. "No," she laughed. "Jesus Christ was born in Bethlehem. Did you not know that?"

I have never heard of Bethlehem, but I did not admit that, and I did not dare ask how old Jesus is in case I am supposed to know that as well.

29 December 1938

A terrible blow. Father has discovered that the money he has been paying to an agent to send back to Poland on our behalf has been stolen. The man my father trusted was a trickster. He has cheated us, taken the payments and disappeared. There is no trace of him anywhere. We (and other families like us) have lost everything. Mama cannot stop crying. She looks all puffy.

"I fear we'll never see our family again, Otto," she repeated over and over.

1939

2 January 1939

Sometimes, I feel that Aunt Lidia would have preferred it if we hadn't come to France and stayed with her and Uncle Adam.

It must be very stressful for her because we have been living with them for over half a year now and Mama is so depressed.

21 January 1939

Excellent news! *Tata* has been offered work at the Hôtel-Dieu Hospital on the Île de la Cité right next to Notre Dame, almost smack in the centre of Paris. It is one of the oldest hospitals in Europe, and Papa is working in a children's emergency unit.

Now, with a legal job, he says, we have the possibility of being accepted as French residents. Mother does not want us to become French residents. I don't care. I just want us to be normal again. I want to go to school and be happy with my friends and have my brother here with us.

It has become clear though that we will not be going home for a long time and we cannot continue to stay here illegally. The wait for Marek and Irina is proving to be far more drawn out than *Tata* had ever anticipated. We have not heard any more news from them.

7 March 1939

Hooray! We have been granted temporary residency papers. They are called *permis de séjour*. These will allow us to stay in France legally for the next six months, until the first week of September. Our good fortune came about because father is a doctor and employed by a hospital. "There is always a need for people working in medicine," he smiled, when he told us the news, "particularly doctors who look after children." I could see from his face, from his eyes, how relieved he is.

I am very proud of him.

14 March 1939

Now that Father is earning a decent wage and our financial worries have calmed a little, we are going to find a home of our own. On a temporary basis, of course. We have not discussed what will happen to us when our six-month residency papers expire. We are all hoping that by then, we will be able to return to Poland.

18 March 1939

I expressed my optimism too soon. Two days ago, Hitler and his Wehrmacht troops – his army – moved into Czechoslovakia and took control of the entire country. Czechoslovakia is our neighbour so Hitler's soldiers could easily march into Poland from there. Uncle Adam and

Father have posted money to Warsaw for Aunt Irina's immediate escape.

March 1939

We have rented an apartment. It is furnished, is quite comfortable and has lots of space, and I have a room of my own! Obviously, when the others arrive from Warsaw, I will have to share, but that will be fine. Our new home is south of the River Seine in a quarter – *quartier* is the French word – called Denfert-Rochereau. Denfert-Rochereau has a large square at its centre dominated by a huge lion statue made out of bronze, and there is a railway station. From its central *place,* many roads lead off in many directions, pointing outwards like a star. Our street is rue Froidevaux, and our lodgings overlook a large walled graveyard known as Montparnasse Cemetery, which is right across the street from us. From our huge front window, I can see over the cemetery walls and down onto alleyways lined with many trees. It doesn't look like a sad place, but rather peaceful.

March 1939

I love where we are and I can walk to school from here. For the first time in a long while, I have a positive feeling about life. Our situation is getting better, and I feel sure that we will have news from Marek and Irina soon and that we will all be together again before the beginning of summer. Even *Matkować* has been busy since our move, tidying, organizing. She took me shopping with her to a nearby street, rue Daguerre. I have never seen such a display of foodstuffs on offer. There were small children with sticks of baguette under their arms running fast, others cradling live chickens, and I saw geese honking from behind wooden box-like pens, and the faces of the vendors were a wonderful sight. The fishmonger had a black wiry moustache as wide and upright as the handlebars on a bicycle.

"Look, Mama, *makrela*!" We often used to eat this fish in Warsaw, buying it fresh from our local market. "Oh, do let's have some, and when we taste it, it will remind us of home."

So Mama bought us three shiny black and silver mackerels as well as all sorts of cheeses and a basket laden with vegetables. She said she is looking forward to cooking lots of our favourite dishes in her new kitchen.

I help her chop vegetables, while tearing off morsels of freshly baked baguette, which is warm and delicious. I try to teach her a few basic words of French, but she just shakes her head. "Listen, *Matkować*," I tell her, "you could shop without me if you could express yourself a little better."

"I prefer to be with you, Rebecca. I don't want to be out alone. I feel too nervous here where we are far from our own kind."

She worries me.

12 April 1939

There is a really nice girl whose parents own our flat. Well, they own the entire building. I think they must be very rich (much richer than Uncle Adam). Her name is Claudette Lautrec, and she has invited me to have tea with her and her family. I have never been invited anywhere for tea before.

14 April 1939

Claudette cancelled our tea date, but said I can come another time. She said her father had told her she must be nice to me. What does that mean? I am not sure I like her all that much now.

17 April 1939

I bumped into Claudette in Montparnasse on my way home from school. She invited me for a lemonade. When I dithered, she laughed at me. "Don't be so afraid," she cried and yanked me by the arm and sat me at a street café. I felt rather nervous in her company. She is very self assured.

"Father says you have run away from your country and that we must be very welcoming to you."

"That's not necessary, thank you," I retorted. "We are very fine and all is well with us."

"Are you poor?" she asked, as she tossed the coins for

our drinks down onto the table and smiled at the waiter as though he were her best friend.

"I don't think so."

"Your clothes are a bit sad. I can give you some blouses and skirts that I've outgrown, if you like. You're much shorter than me, but Helena, our maid, can take up the hems for you."

"No, thank you, I have plenty. Excuse me, I must go."

"Let's walk together," she insisted.

Well, I could hardly refuse as she had just bought me lemonade and citron tart. In fact, as we began to stroll along the main boulevard, she seemed a bit nicer, less stuck up. She has no brothers or sisters, she told me. I didn't mention Marek because I didn't want her to say something bad about *Tata*, accusing him of having left half our family behind.

"What are your hobbies?" she wanted to know. "What will you do when you leave school, or do you just want to get married?"

"Married?! I haven't given it a thought."

What a curious question.

"I want to be a famous actress," she whispered as though it were a very daring secret. "But my parents think that is quite awful."

I found her a bit difficult to talk to. Still, she is very beautiful. People notice her in the street and it is only partly because she throws her arms about so frequently and is very animated.

20 April 1939

Claudette arrived at our front door with a huge brown parcel. It was for me and contained two blouses and a swinging floral-patterned skirt. The blouses are a bit long but tucked inside my other clothes you cannot really notice. The skirt has been taken up and fits me perfectly. Mama said I am to be very nice to our neighbour for her kindness, but I feel awkward and I have nothing to give her in return.

22 April 1939

I wrote Claudette a thank-you note and left it at the end of our cobbled cul-de-sac with the concierge.

I haven't heard back.

1 May 1939

Today is May Day or Labour Day. It is a public holiday.

On the street corners or at makeshift stalls, women with their small boys in short trousers and long socks and berets on their heads or old men with big stomachs in check shirts and braces, every kind of working person, are selling small pots of lily of the valley. *Muguet* the French call this very delicate flower.

Claudette invited me to tea again, and this time she did not cancel. Their house is very grand, and the tea was served in a silver teapot with matching milk jug. The table with a white linen cloth was dressed with several pots of *muguet*s. My school friend told me that young men offer these white flowers, the tiny lilies, as a gift to the girl of their choice. It is a declaration of love.

"Don't you think that is very romantic? When I am a famous actress, I will receive many bunches and pots," she grinned.

I laughed out loud at her because I did not take her seriously. For a moment, I feared she was about to be very cross and then she burst out laughing too.

"You look very pretty in that skirt." She smiled and hugged me hard. "I like you. Shall we be best friends and tell each other all our secrets?"

10 May 1939

It is my birthday. Twelve today.

Claudette found a map of Europe and the Mediterranean Sea. It was a special supplement in one of last year's editions of *National Geographic* magazine. It was on sale down near the Quai Montebello not far from Notre Dame. Its original price was fifty cents, that is half a US dollar, but she bought it for eighty-five francs from one of the small bookstalls that line the riverbank and then gave it to me as a birthday present. We strolled by the stalls; all selling second-hand books, some quite rare editions, prints, drawings, photographs, illustrations and maps. These stallholders are known as *bouquinistes* and their goods are laid out in boxes or on wooden structures either side of the upper walkways that flank the Seine. Today, we walked from Quai d'Orsay on the Left Bank all the way east past the cathedral to the Jardin des Plantes, the Botanical Gardens. The booksellers themselves are a curious sight too. Many are perched on small wooden stools, backs facing the river, looking out towards the main thoroughfare. Some wear floppy hats, others have big walrus moustaches, many smoke long curled pipes and they all look very intellectual!

Afterwards, we walked to the Boulevard Saint-Germain and drank hot chocolate at the Café de Flore. I felt very grown-up sitting out on the terrace with my stylish friend, watching the automobiles pass by and the dozens of different types seated within the café, smoking very smelly cigarettes and drinking small glasses of wine or cognac.

"Do you smoke?" Claudette asked me suddenly, biting into a *petit* almond macaroon, a dish of which were served with our hot chocolates.

"Smoke? Of course not!"

"But have you tried it?"

"No, never." I was completely taken aback by my friend's questions. "Have you?"

"Maybe. I'm not telling. Come on, let's go. I'll be late for dinner and *Maman* will nag me."

Sometimes I feel so much younger than Claudette, even though there is only a year and a bit between us. I am thrilled with her gift though. It is perfect because even though I cannot read the English text (not yet, but Claudette can and she translated bits for me), I can study the countries of Europe and try to understand a little more precisely all that is happening in our homeland and with the Germans. And I can see how far from Warsaw we are!

20 May 1939

Claudette told me that her parents have a house by the sea near Italy. They visit there for the summer holidays, for months at a time. I cannot believe they would go all that distance just for their holidays. It is miles away!

It's nice to be alone with my diary. Like visiting a friend I haven't seen in a while. I have so little time for it these days. There is so much to do, including writing up my homework in French. It makes the task even longer, but my French is getting really fluent. Claudette says I speak it almost as well as she does. That is not quite true, but it boosts my confidence.

27 May 1939

Claudette was talking to me about a new film festival that has been inaugurated near where her family have their house in the south of France. It is held in Cannes, and she says that next year we must go there together and never go to school but watch lots of films. "A cinema festival right on our doorstep. Films all day long, just imagine it!" She seems very excited about it all.

June 1939

Still no news from Warsaw. Everyone is worried.

2 July 1939

Claudette says we must go and see a film called *The Wizard of Oz*.

26 July 1939

Marek's birthday. He is three today.

Claudette and her parents left Paris a few days ago for their house down in the south. I really miss her. We have been spending lots of time together and now I feel lonely and miserable. Having her around is like having a sister. Now that Claudette has gone, I really want to go back to Poland. I miss my baby brother and my friends.

Mama has a very bad cough. I can hear her at night. She never stops, like a goose, honking and honking.

20 August 1939

Father has applied for an extension on our residency papers. He has been told we must wait. "Come back on the expiry date," the official said to him. We don't know what we are waiting for, or how long it will take but our status is becoming uncertain again.

Claudette and her family are still away. No news from her and no news from home either.

We had dinner with Uncle Adam and Aunt Lidia. Delicious food as always. A great big sizzling duck *à l'orange*. After our meal, while the others were out in the conservatory talking, Lidia played records on her phonograph for me. I liked one very jolly tune called, "*Chanson Gîtane*" ("*Gypsy Song*").

What fun it would be to own such an instrument and to make music whenever I felt like it. Lidia said that Hitler despises gypsies as much as Jews. I confided in her how afraid I am for Marek and Aunt Irina. She held my hand and told me that all will be well. These things take time but Hitler will be stopped, she assured me. I hope she is right.

1 September 1939

It cannot be true, but it is! Germany has invaded Poland. It is impossible to make any contact with home and it is a horrible, horrible time. What are we doing so far from our roots and away from my brother? Why did we leave, why has Father broken up the family? Marek is three now. He must be walking and talking yet all my images of him are as a gurgling baby. This evening, I wanted to shout at *Tata*, take us home, why don't you? But it seems there will be no going home. To reunite us as a family, our only hope is to secure the exit of Aunt Irina and Marek. But how, when we seem to have lost contact with them?

3 September 1939

It was a warm, sunny Sunday morning and we had been intending to go out for a walk along by the river, but Father said we should stay home and switch on the wireless set. We sat together in the drawing room of our first-floor flat with its big picture windows overlooking the graveyard. The British Prime Minister, his name is Neville Chamberlain, came over the airwaves, crackly and very serious.

"I am speaking to you from the Cabinet Room at 10, Downing Street." (That's in London.)

Only my father could understand the English words, and he translated for us as the man spoke. I will never forget that announcement and the tone of that foreigner's solemn voice.

"This morning the British Ambassador in Berlin handed the German Government a final note stating that unless we heard from them by 11.00 a.m. that they were prepared at once to withdraw their troops from Poland, a state of war would exist between us.

"I have to tell you that no such undertaking has been received, and that consequently this country is at war with Germany."

"War has been declared," murmured *Tata*.

What has it got to do with England? I wanted to know. Father explained softly that France and Britain are friends with Poland and if our country is in danger, they have promised to defend us.

I felt so sick. Even though some people said it would happen, the fact that it is real… War. What will it mean?

Mr Chamberlain went on to say that Hitler would not entertain any discussions for a peaceful settlement between his country and Poland.

"So, no peace for Poland, no returning?" my mother said to my father. He settled his hand across both of hers, clasped tightly together in her lap. She looked like a damaged bird.

"Where are they?" she wept. "Why have we heard nothing?"

Chamberlain continued. "We and France are today, in fulfilment of our obligations, going to the aid of Poland, who is bravely resisting this wicked and unprovoked attack on her people…"

4 September 1939

Everything I grew up with seems so out of reach, almost alien, as though I dreamt that first life then went to sleep and woke up in another body with unrelated things all around me. Poland, poor Poland, but above all, my poor brother and auntie. I watched the concern on my parents' faces yesterday morning and then again in the late afternoon when we learned that France was backing Britain and has also declared war on Germany. Having travelled hundreds and hundreds of miles to flee danger, we now find ourselves living in a war zone and separated from members of our family.

5 September 1939

Our temporary residency papers officially expired today. Father returned to request a renewal and was told again that we must wait, that we are living under extraordinary circumstances and new rules will apply.

6 September 1939

Given the appalling change in national circumstances, Claudette and her parents have cut short the last week of their holiday and returned to Paris. I was so pleased to see her. Her skin is glowing and dark from being out in the sun and she looks so healthy, like a beautiful gypsy. Apparently, her parents own a vast farm where they grow grapes and make wine. She said her parents are very concerned for us. Her father is worried for our safety. Do we have the correct papers? she asked me. I shrugged and said I didn't know. Father went to talk with Uncle Adam this evening, to see if he can help speed up the renewal of our documents.

The American president, Mr Roosevelt, has announced that America will remain neutral and not join the war.

What is going to happen to everybody? People talk of nothing but "the impending war".

21st September 1939

The situation back home in Warsaw is getting worse. Poland has surrendered to the Germans.

I have been so busy and worried that I did not note down here that we started school again two weeks ago. Montparnasse is not at all far from our apartment, I can walk there by myself. The new class I have joined – because my French is much better – has thirteen girls and nine boys. There are three other foreigners like me, but they are all French-speaking. Well, I am French-speaking too!

28th September 1939

Our homeland has officially been declared a conquered state, jointly ruled by Germany from the west and the Soviet Union, who have entered from the east. Mother begged *Tata* to take us home. It was all she could talk about. She blamed him for our situation and her mood was very argumentative. If he will not take her back, she has threatened to make her own way to Warsaw. That's nonsense, of course. Since we've been here, she has become too scared to even go to the shops alone, but even if she got through Germany, which is totally impossible, she would not be allowed across the border. None of us would be. Poland is closing its borders to all Jews, even Polish Jews who are living abroad. Our situation is worse than ever before because if our visas are not renewed, we will become stateless. We will be refugees living in a war zone who belong nowhere and have no citizens' rights. I cannot think about it, it is too terrifying.

November 1939

News!! A letter has arrived at Uncle Adam's house! It was sent by a colleague of Father's from the hospital where he worked in Warsaw. It says that it is believed that my brother and aunt fled the country almost a year ago and are living in Lithuania. They escaped with a small party of fellow Jews who managed to make their way over the border. As far as the author of the letter knows, they are safe. What a relief, if this information is accurate. The downside is that they are even further away from us than they were before. (I looked on my map.) How will we ever be reunited?

School is good. I have made one or two friends in my class, but no one special yet. The other foreigners are Hans and Jacob from Germany. They are twin brothers. Also, there is a girl called Miriam. She is older, fourteen, but because her French is not so good she is in our class. I think she is from Austria. She doesn't say much, seems very shy. They are all Jewish and left their countries for the same reasons we did. We don't discuss it though. It's better to keep quiet about the past and the circumstances that have brought us here. Both Father and Uncle Adam have warned me to be discreet and disclose as little as possible.

November 1939

Yet again Father has applied for an extension on our residents' papers. Again he has been told we must wait. We have no idea how long the wait will be. Claudette asked me if we wanted to spend Christmas with her and her family. She laughed when I told her, "Don't be silly, we are Jewish." "So?" she riposted. "Who cares, you can still come and have a Christmas meal with us. We are not going to poison you!"

3 December 1939

There is nothing else we can do during these short winter days in Paris but live our lives and try not to dwell on the war. In any case, it does not seem to exist. Nothing has happened. I go to school and I enjoy the walk through the city streets, and then I come home and work on my French and my homework. It's all quite normal. Nothing war-like about any of my days. Our lives continue in as ordinary a fashion as possible.

It rained all day. I stayed in and read.

10 December 1939

At the weekends, if Father is not working at the hospital or is not booked with private patients, he and I cross the river to the Louvre. Today was our third visit there. It is the most wonderful art gallery in the world. From there, we strolled to the Jewish quarter situated in a district known as le Marais.

I love these outings. We frequently make a pause, to drink cups of black coffee or buy Viennese pastries from one of the many delicious *pâtisseries* tucked away in the narrow lanes, squeezed in between dozens of tailoring shops. We never talk in Polish. My French is as good as Papa's now, and sometimes we even speak a few words together in English. *Tata* encourages me with my languages, particularly French because he believes it is essential that I can pass for a French girl. "It could become necessary," he says.

Necessary in what way? But he is never more specific.

It is only at home with *Matkować* that we speak Polish. She never comes with us on these outings. She prefers to stay in the house and do needlework.

December 1939

I love Paris, and when I am not missing my baby brother and Warsaw, I am happy here. I even like it here when it rains even though I dread that something really bad is going to happen to us soon. I cannot describe what it is that I dread, but sometimes I feel as though a big black spectre is looming over me, waiting to grab hold of me, waiting to pounce.

17 December 1939

Father is working today so we cannot go to the Louvre or set out on one of our exploratory walks together.

Last night, Claudette and I went to a picture show at the Cinémathèque Française. I have never been to such a place before. It was packed and was astounding. We watched a story called *L'Atalante*. This was the film Aunt Lidia talked to me about, the one with that beautiful song she played so frequently. The story was very romantic and quite sad in parts. When the two main characters became separated, I really wept because it reminded me of our broken family. Claudette teased me afterwards and said I was soft. She said that when she is older, she wants to fall in love and go off with her husband on a boat like the lovers in the film or just far away from her family.

"I thought you wanted to be an actress."

"Actresses can marry, and you take everything I say so literally. I am dreaming!"

"Are you unhappy?" I asked her, amazed.

"No, silly. I just want adventure. I want to travel, to see places and meet people."

"Not yet."

"Sssh, please don't fret, my Rebecca. We will be reunited with your brother and Aunt Irina before too long. Or, as soon as we can, we will join them in the United States." Father was attempting to cheer us up again. "At some point, the way forward will become clear, my little robin. We must have faith. We must trust."

I wonder. I don't know what to hope for any longer or what to believe.

I have never doubted my father before, never in my life, but I do now.

27 March 1940

I should rip this diary up. It is wicked to mistrust my own father, who is such a good man and has everyone's best interests at heart. He would be mortified were he to read what I have written.

Early April 1940

We are not the only ones living in limbo land for although war has been declared, nothing at all has happened. All of Paris, indeed all of France, seems to be sitting on the edge of its seat, waiting, picturing the future, debating about what it might hold. So, the French are rather like us now, staring into an uncertain darkness.

And we still have no renewal on our residency papers.

Life goes on. At school, I have been learning some French history. It is quite different to our Polish past. What a proud and powerful nation France has been. While our country seems always to have been occupied by others, France has been an imperial power ruling over many nations. Its language has been taught all over the world and has been the language of the educated in many of the courts of kings and queens. Russia, for example, before it was communist, when it was ruled by Tsars.

10 May 1940

After months of tension and no activity, after a drawn-out political stalemate in Europe that has become known as the "*Sitzkriek*", the "*drôle de guerre*", or, in English, the "phoney war", Germany has invaded France.

And guess what, world, it's my thirteenth birthday! Thank you, Mr Hitler.

Chaos has broken out everywhere, all at once. Trains are jam-packed with refugees from Germany, Belgium and Holland. All pouring into the Paris railway stations. Mostly Jews, just like us – thousands of others are now trying to get into France, to settle here. Everybody wants to escape Hitler's armies who are now intent upon reaching the French capital.

This influx of foreigners will make the renewal of our papers even more complicated and slow.

14 May 1940

Claudette has invited me to go south with her and her parents to spend the summer at Mérivel, their house by the sea. I didn't say anything and I haven't mentioned it to my parents. Life's easy for her. She has nothing to be afraid of. I have to battle with myself sometimes not to feel jealous.

30 May 1940

Northern France has been doing its upmost to defend itself against the invading German armies, but the reports are that many French soldiers have been taken prisoner. Many have died, and the enemy is moving forwards, drawing closer to the capital.

And we still have no papers. I wish my mother had taken the time to learn French. There's no concealing where she comes from. On top of which, if we have to escape again, her illness will make the going more hazardous. I wish I could just run off by myself. It's hard not to hate what has happened to my life. Am I being horribly selfish?

3 June 1940

Bombs were dropped on Paris this evening. Mama was at the hospital for an X-ray. I was alone in the house, sitting in the kitchen after school, eating an apple, concentrating on my homework. What alerted me were the sounds of planes overhead. Not one single drone, but several in quick succession. I leapt from my chair and hurried to take a look. In the distance, I could see flames leaping up out of a series of buildings alongside the river. I shoved open the window – it was still warm outside – my senses were hit by the sweet scent of the horse chestnut blossoms in the cemetery across the street and also a horrid rubbery smell. It was something burning. Beneath me, people were running in the street, shouting. "*Nous sommes envahis*," they cried. "We are being invaded." "*Paris brûle*." "Paris is burning." One man in a striped suit was weeping, blubbing like a baby.

"Is the whole city on fire?" I yelled loudly, but no one answered me. I was so afraid the flames would reach our street before my parents came home. Are they safe? Is the hospital an engulfed, burning mass? I was running crazily about the sitting room, trying to think what I should do, opening all windows, crawling out on to the ledge as far as I could, looking, calling for my parents, scanning the skyline for fire and bombs.

4 June 1940

Bombs again, soon after dawn. We were getting dressed in the dark, fumbling about because there was a blackout. I could hear sirens wailing from far away. They sounded like the cries of Marek when he was first born. Wailing and incessant. And gunfire. It was very scary. My hands were trembling as I stepped into my skirt and laced up my shoes. Father came knocking on my door. "Try not to be afraid," he whispered. Why whisper? As though the planes far overhead might hear our exchanges.

5 June 1940

Thousands of people are fleeing the capital now. It is not only foreigners and Jews like us, but also the French. It is pandemonium.

On my way home from school this afternoon I waited back in the street in the shade of a tall plane tree, observing families charging out of their doors, loading up carts with their possessions, hurling objects here and there, yelling at one another, kicking dogs, tossing them into cars. Vehicles, heavy with furniture strapped to every last bit of the carcass, were crawling along the streets like overladen beasts. The cars' interiors were jammed with families and their dogs, cats, sharp-yellow canary birds in cages, children bawling their heads off.

Where are they all going?

6 June 1940

We spend our time with ears against the wireless, seated in silence. I have started chewing nervously at my lip, which makes my mother mad at me. I have started biting my nails, too. They look horrid.

Thousands and thousands of ordinary French citizens are trying to escape from many areas of the north to beat a path south. We are hearing on the wireless that the cities south of here have been swamped. The inhabitants cannot handle this mass invasion of their own people. The railway stations have queues that snake back miles. Lines of flustered folk with suitcases and too many belongings. The world seems to be going mad, moving south, without any real sense of where they are intended.

"What about us, *Tata*?" I begged.

"We'll stay, Rebecca," he assured me. "I will be needed at the hospital, now more than ever, and Ruby is not strong enough to travel, not just yet."

Thank heavens we will not be caught up within the agitated crowds.

7 June 1940

We are leaving! Father has changed his mind.

He explained that 245 people have been killed during the bombings of Paris. Twenty were children. He has decided that we must get out before the Germans flood the capital, but where will we go? We still have no papers. That is all the more reason why we must leave, he claims.

Claudette's father paid us a visit this evening. He seemed keen to help. Claudette was with him. She was crying.

"Where are you going?" she sobbed. It was curious to see her in such a state; she is usually so in control.

"I don't know. There is no plan. We haven't made any preparations."

Preparations or not, we are leaving at first light.

Pre-dawn 8 June 1940

Almost no sleep. Parents in next room gathering precious possessions together, such as we have. Mother making some food for the road. I am scribbling, writing fast and by candlelight, hands trembling just a little from apprehension.

I feel a need to repeat this information in case anything happens to me, to us... I am Rebecca Mortkowicz. This country is France. I have torn a map out of my school atlas and glued it into my diary, which I am about to secrete at the very bottom of my lovely leather satchel. My diary is Top Secret. If anything should happen to me... Why do I repeat this?

Oh, my thoughts are so unsettled, irrational.

Before hiding my book of scribblings, I have circled Paris with a pencil. Paris, from where this second journey, our second flight, is commencing. Wherever we go, there will be no wonderful Uncle Adam to take us in and offer us refuge. We will be out there in the world running and friendless.

8 June 1940

We are on the move, southwards towards a warmer climate. Nothing planned or carefully thought through. Unlike the first time we made our escape, this time we are not travelling alone. The roads, towns, cities all the way to the southern half of France are snarled up in a chaos of moving traffic, both human and other. I can sometimes glimpse the trundling lines from the train windows. Although my view is blocked most of the time by the hordes of anxious bodies squeezed up against me. We don't even know where we are going. We just grabbed places on the first train offering even minimal space. All we have been told by others aboard is that it is descending south, but where exactly is anybody's guess.

"Better for your mama's health," Papa encouraged as we pushed and shoved to climb on board.

We are just following the queues of terrified people. We are a part of them now, a part of the mass hysteria.

The train is moving at a snail's pace. Stop, start. Stop, start. Full of flies and broken hearts. We are packed together like herds of cattle. People are sobbing and sniffing, some are retching. It is ghastly. My senses are so attuned to everything

I can even hear silence; the others' silence. The silence of loss, of not knowing when life will be normal again. The unspoken questions about why all this is happening to us. I am beginning to believe I can even smell silence.

So many bodies pressed tightly up against one another, all control of life and our daily functions snatched away from us.

10 June 1940

Throughout our arduous journey, which has lasted over two days so far, I have caught only fleeting glimpses of my parents. Father is clutching mother. She clings to him most of the time, grabbing at his clothes. Clamped together in the corridor, she resembles a puppet whose strings have been snipped, who has grown floppy and lifeless. I shove my face hard against the windowpane whenever I can, desperate to catch the names of the stations, some at which we stop and others where we limp through at the pace of a sick animal.

I overhear people asking their travelling companions when they are intending to go back home, but I have stopped asking such a question. I say to myself, repeating it if I don't believe myself, "there is no back home". I invented it or dreamed it. Home has become the unknown. Home is the graveyard opposite our flat in rue Froidevaux. I remember it covered in snow earlier this year. I try to picture what Claudette is doing now, and I wonder why the Lautrecs are safe and we are not...

The further, the deeper, we descend, the more silent people become. No one seems to have the will for words or even for thoughts.

11 June 1940

The scent of tightly packed, unwashed bodies is making me really nauseous. I spotted a sign a while ago, which read Clermont-Ferrand but I cannot look now to see where that is because I am squashed into this compartment and cannot reach my leather bag or my coat. They are perched on my feet and there is no room to bend down.

We could be anywhere in the world. What difference does it make?

12 June 1940

We have reached the south. The train has stopped and everyone, stretching aching limbs, has been disembarking so I suppose this is the end of the line. The station sign reads Montpelier but where exactly that is I am not yet sure. (As soon as I can, I will look at my map). The climate is hot. The sun is beating against my skin, which itches because I badly need a wash. We are all too exhausted to speak, to form words, to make decisions. My throat and mouth ache from thirst. What now? Why ask? Does it matter any more?

14 June 1940

After two days in this cramped *pension* in this city of Montpelier, Father has taken the decision to move us on again. "Why?" Both my mother and I hotly protested. "There are loads of other refugees here. We're safe."

Papa disagrees. German soldiers have marched into Paris,

he says. French citizens are weeping in the streets of the capital. Hitler's flag, with a swastika on it, is flying from the Eiffel Tower. The French are defeated. If the German troops keep on moving and penetrate this far south, here, there, anywhere where foreigners have settled, these will be the first places the Wehrmacht will look. All temporary ghettoes, they will root out, rip apart. Any cluster of Poles, the finger will be pointed. Polish Jewish refugees on the run, that is what we are and there are thousands of other families just like us, all looking for work, all searching for a means to survive, all trying to hide. Nazi Germany has caused this upheaval. If we stay here, we will be pushed into a corner from where there will be no escape and then they will round us up, as they have been doing in Germany, and shoot or imprison us.

15 June 1940

We have decided, or Father has, that we will go it alone, as we did at the very beginning of this odyssey, travelling under our own steam, very discreetly because our short-term permits are months out of date, until we find an ordinary, unassuming French village and there we will install ourselves in a tiny *pension* and recuperate for a few weeks. He and I both have perfect French so that will assist us. We will be able to blend in easily with the locals, do the shopping at the markets, keep a low profile. Mama, not. She's the risk. Poor *Matkować*.

Tata has told me that he has Monsieur Lautrec's holiday address memorized, just in case. Nothing written down, just in case.

"Claudette's father has given you their address? But they are still in Paris. Do we have a key?"

"They have staff working there and we will be made welcome. But it will not be necessary. This war will soon be over, everyone claims it. Life in France will be back to normal very soon."

17 June 1940

We are travelling east, mostly on trains, always staying close to the coast. People are saying that we will be shown more kindness closer to Italy, but how to get there? And to *where* precisely? The journey is very long and I never stop reminding myself that we have no papers. If we are stopped and searched, we will be arrested. And then what?

The scenery is very different here, beautiful. The sea is

turquoise at the water's edge and then becomes a blinding blue extending to its horizon. It helps me breathe, elates me, gives me hope. Somewhere beyond all this water … lies what? A new life? There is a land I cannot see on the far side of this sea where some Jews have escaped to. The Promised Land. Palestine. The home of our ancestors and our gospels. I close my eyes and try to picture it. The same land where Claudette says her Christ was born in Bethlehem. He was a Jew. That is very curious to me. The Nazis who hunt us are Christians and their God was a Jew. I cannot understand why they hate us then. It's illogical.

I have never set eyes on the sea before today. It is thrilling to watch the landscape unfold and slip away as we inch towards Italy, yet always the water hugging close to us. It glitters beneath the sun's glare and looks friendly and inviting, and sometimes when we leave the train to visit a seaside village, to spend the night, I am spellbound by the sounds I hear: the wind playing gently in the giant trees, the waves wrapping themselves about the feet of the big bouldered rocks, village dogs barking in the streets. Are they barking because they know we are strangers; because we are Jews?

In spite of the war, life here appears normal. Without fear. The buildings are not protected by sandbags, nothing is in short supply, and when the train crawls through the small towns, where many of the houses are painted bright colours, there are locals out shopping, strolling about the streets as though they have nothing to be afraid of, as though this is a different country altogether. Elsewhere. I watch the women, two and three abreast, with woven baskets, laughing, smiling. One caught my eye, dark-haired, rather young. She waved and I waved back.

In between the towns, there lies miles of deserted coastline. No properties or buildings at all, no people, only jutting impressive rocks, sea and sand dunes, craggy narrow promontories like grasping claws and sometimes sheer-faced cliffs. Occasionally, I spot a group of children splashing and diving-bombing in the water. Such explosions of energy. To be so carefree, I hardly remember such a time. And then the train curves and leans and we snake towards a wide gaping bay where tiny figures are sprinting along the sand and middle-aged men in hats are seated on wooden chairs at the water's edge, fishing, munching on baguette sandwiches.

I pass these long sticky hours, sweat rolling down my back, jotting down my thoughts, my impressions, my observations, as I am doing now, or I simply stare out of the window, transfixed. Any distraction is better than listening to mother's hacking cough. All this travelling has weakened her. As soon as she walks more than a few yards, she is breathless and starts coughing again and her skin becomes tacky and almost transparent.

Father warned me that I must be patient with Mama, because she is ailing. Ailing, such a curious word. What does it mean precisely? Is ailing more serious than being exhausted and sad? Is it a special kind of sickness that includes shadows on her lungs? Is a shadow an illness?

Poor mother. I believe though that when we find a real place to settle and move into a home of our own, she will get better, and be back to her old self. The climate here will be very healing for her and life will be good again. That's what Father says and I have to believe it.

21 June 1940

We have reached the port town of Nice. It is miles from all troubles, they say. Here, we have been told, we will be safe, we will be shown kindness. I can hardly believe that throughout all these days on the road, we have managed to avoid all checks for identification papers. What good fortune. Rare good fortune.

According to the directions given to Papa by Mr Lautrec we are about thirty kilometres from Claudette's holiday home.

Is that where we are going? I asked Father.

"We'll see. We'll discuss that problem tomorrow. Today we are going to have a huge fish meal down at the waterfront and stay one night in a *pension*."

The page from my atlas indicates that we have travelled hundreds of kilometres along the Mediterranean coast. Nice is quite close to Italy. It is much smaller than Montpelier. It looks really pretty, rather exotic and as far as we can judge, it is calm and safe. The scents are more powerful, quite overwhelming, sweeter. They almost make me feel giddy mixed in with the salty sea air. The flowers are vibrant colours – purples, golden-yellow, scarlet red – climbing up walls everywhere as though they can't stay still, and the leaves appear to be bigger having gorged themselves on heat and light.

All we need now is somewhere to sleep, which my father has set out to find while I wait down at the harbour with our luggage and mother, my *Matkować*, who has grown so terribly thin and pale.

22 June 1940

We searched all day yesterday, but the lodgings and small hotels are very expensive here and the little money we have will have to last until Father finds work or until we return to Paris. Eventually, when it was getting a bit late and mother was exhausted from moving about in the heat, we decided to go in search of Mérivel, the Lautrec's house. Claudette did not tell me the truth. She was being very modest. It is not a holiday house at all. It is an enormous estate with its main house more like a mansion. On the land are several houses. Field after field of vines. Orchards of fruit trees: peaches, almonds, lemons and terraced rows of another tree, silvery and knobbly. This is the olive tree. I have never seen such a tree before.

Michel Haricot is the caretaker, the *gardien*. His name made me giggle. It means "bean" and he's such a plump squat fellow, all bunched up like a broad bean, with the most extraordinary accent – twangy and difficult to understand. He was very kind and did not seem surprised that we have turned up. He showed us immediately to a pretty cottage. It's not a huge space, but it is for our sole occupancy and we can stay as long as we need to and we have a view of the sea from its front porch. It's wonderful. I have fallen in love with the place already.

Our new home has three rooms and a kitchen and bathroom so I can still have my own room. Nearby, there is a village, also called Mérivel. It is not much but somewhere to buy bread. A little further along the coast there is a seaside town and there are schools in Nice. I will attend the classes there, starting as soon as possible so that I don't fall behind in my studies. Once we know what our future holds, we'll find a more permanent situation. Father intends to either set himself up as a paediatrician and work from the cottage, but that will be jolly cramped and a bit isolated for visitors, or he will apply for a post at the hospital in Nice. If not, he will attempt to join a medical practice.

Montpelier to Nice is 275 kilometres. Obviously not as long a journey as Warsaw to Paris but nerve-racking.

I can only describe our mood as joyous, elated, although we are all too tired to appreciate anything more than relief. Relief, yes, because for a while at least we are safe, we have found ourselves an area where we will not be hunted and arrested nor forced to move on.

23 June 1940

The news is that France has surrendered to Germany. The swastika flag is flown everywhere about the capital, the French flag has been lowered. Hitler himself is in the capital with his troops. It seems the French prefer the Germans to inhabit and rule this country rather than destroy its buildings and its history.

The Germans we met during our escape from Poland to France, those that Father calls the "ordinary people", were mostly quite nice so I don't suppose it will be too ghastly. On the other hand, those that have invaded Poland, the soldiers, seem to be utterly horrid. But they are the army, the Wehrmacht, so perhaps that is the difference. The real problem begins with their leader, Adolf Hitler, who hates Jews and gypsies and wants to take everyone else's country to build a bigger empire for himself.

24 June 1940

German soldiers with their tanks have been arriving into Paris from every direction. The villagers here are speaking about nothing else. Thank heavens we have escaped. Father was right to take us out of the capital, even if the upheaval has been exhausting for Mother. She has been in bed since we arrived. Her coughing is a bit frightening. I hope it gets better soon.

The estate manager and his wife, Monsieur and Madame Fournier, have a son. His name is Robert. He walked over to our cottage this afternoon to say hello and to invite me up to the stables to see the horses. Claudette's parents keep five here and one, Belle, is ridden exclusively by Robert when Claudette is not here. Robert has no brothers or sisters. He is sixteen, so a bit older than me but he seems friendly. He thought it odd that I have never been on a horse. As we were walking across the fields, all planted up with young, green vine stock, he quizzed me about my background and where we had come from. I immediately clamped up. I would like us to be friends but I prefer not to say too much. Father has warned me over and over about discussing our background. We are not ashamed of our Jewish heritage, he always makes clear, but we need to guard it close to ourselves. I crossed my fingers behind my back and told Robert that we are from Paris and had left when the bombs began to fall close to our home and that we want to be in a better climate for my mother's health. He frowned but didn't ask any more questions. I wonder if my accent gives me away.

There are no signs of war here, he said, and I have seen none. The horses are magnificent. Belle, Robert's favourite horse, is a mare the colours of treacle and milk.

"You can see you're from the city," he laughed when I shied away from the mare's chewing mouth, all whiskery and slobbery with big chomping teeth. I thought she was going to bite me. I felt hurt to be laughed at. Robert is very confident and extremely handsome. Tall and handsome. He moves with ease and to watch him just climb up onto the horse and gallop it straight from the stables … well, I was a bit breathless.

Do I like Robert Fournier? Yes, I do.

12 July 1940

France has been divided up into two parts. The north and west, including the entire Atlantic coast, is to be governed by the German Wehrmacht, and to be known as the *Zone occupée*. The new French president, an old soldier called Marshall Pétain, along with his government, who will be based in Vichy, a town halfway down the country, will rule the southern half of France, all the way to Italy. This is to be known as the French State, *État Français*. It has been designated a Free Zone, unoccupied territory, which means unoccupied by the Germans. We have landed up in a distant part of the zone NOT occupied by Germans and we are SO fortunate because we are well out of their reach here. We can relax and rebuild our lives. We have nothing left to fear.

Robert invited me to go swimming after school but I felt a bit shy so made the excuse that I have heaps of homework. His mother told him that Claudette will be coming here with her parents in a day or two. I cannot wait to see her again.

25 July 1940

Claudette arrived and I am having the finest of summers. Now I have two gorgeous and very grown-up friends. Robert is a bit less confident when we are in the company of Claudette. They seem to be very close and I felt a bit jealous watching the pair of them off riding together, but at least I have plucked up the courage to go to the beach with them. However, they are both very gay and frolicsome and it makes me feel a bit of a downbeat frump.

Still, the sky is bluer than I ever imagined a sky could be and we laze on the sand in the shade of large round boulders that burn our flesh if we accidently rub against them. We read, we talk, we dream and we eat masses. I think that if I were here without my parents I would have forgotten my Polish altogether. I never talk about my past and our journeys to get here, no matter how many questions my two new friends ask me.

"Best forgotten," I mutter, though I don't mean that.

I have been learning to swim. Robert says I am a natural, "a fish", and then, when I'm tired out and my skin has been cooled by the sea, I flop onto the sand with my eyes closed and listen to the gentle whoosh of the waves against the pebbles and the sand. I like the sting, the pinch of the salt drying and puckering my skin, which is turning the colour of pale wood.

Some days we take bicycles and ride inland to picnic beyond the estate vineyards from where we pluck great swinging bunches of tart grapes, gorging on them in the shade of tall, feathery eucalyptus trees till they give us stomach ache. There are funny little insects, cicadas, that you almost never see but you certainly hear them; they screech like angry violins from dawn to nightfall. They are the sound of summer in Provence, says Robert. Summer in Provence. I could never have imagined that there was a place like this anywhere in the world. Nowhere could be better and the knowledge that we are out of reach of the war and far from the clutch of the Germans makes our lives all the sweeter.

As soon as we have news from Aunt Irina and Marek, Father is going to write to them to come to us here. This is where we will build our future life, not America, he has decided. Even mother is a little better. I simply could not be happier.

26 July 1940

Marek's fourth birthday ... nothing to say on this subject!

4 August 1940

How I enjoy lying spread-eagled in the scorched grass, my back scratched and torn by the rough dry earth, because it hasn't rained for months, watching eagles circling overhead as they silently turn on broad wings, waiting until they make that special call that eagles make, that wistful whistling. I close my eyes and believe that their plaint can be heard all the way across Europe. Messengers of sadness, pipers of the gap that grows inside you when you are worn away by longing, and yet I am not unhappy. I love it here and I envy Robert because this is his land. He is a native, a Provençal. He grew up with all this and he takes it all for granted. I feel sure that neither he nor Claudette could ever understand the fear that I live with, the fear of having everything I hold dear snatched away from me.

This is the ghost that haunts me. Even more so now because Mother has been taken ill. She had a strange turn in the night. Father asked Mr Haricot to drive them to the hospital in Nice. I don't understand, she seemed to be getting better a few days ago.

August 1940

Horrible news! The new government in Vichy has decreed that foreigners cannot be employed in certain jobs including the medical profession. Father is not allowed to practise as a doctor anymore, not even here in the unoccupied zone. What are we going to do?

Matkować, my darling mother, has been admitted into a ward at the hospital.

25 August 1940

I read in a French newspaper today that Jewish refugees in Lithuania without diplomatic visas to cross international borders are being forced to stay within the communist-controlled state. We have no idea whether Aunt Irina and Marek have managed to find passage on a boat to America or whether they are still somewhere there, in the capital, Vilnius, perhaps. We are now entirely cut off from them. We have to hope that Uncle Adam will send us their news, if he receives any.

Father says the tests they have done on Mother are "worrying". I went with him to the hospital to see her this evening and I hardly recognized her. Her face has become hollow and her skin is as pale as a lily of the valley flower. *Tata* and I sat side by side, shoulder to shoulder, on the bus coming home to Mérivel, but we barely said a word to one another. I didn't dare ask him any questions. His eyes looked too bleak.

I don't dare write down the sickening thoughts I am thinking, nor write of the spectre I see beckoning.

I was feeling so happy. I must never allow myself to believe in the possibility of happiness. It is a false state of being, at least it is for me. Happiness belongs to those who are more privileged than me, like Claudette and her family, or even Robert.

9 September 1940

Father has been helping Robert's parents on the land. There are a great many preparations for the upcoming grape harvest. I will lend a hand too when I am not at the *lycée*. Father says it's a positive way to contribute; a small opportunity to say thank you for the kindnesses we are being shown. If he cannot work as a doctor, he says, he will offer his strength as a land labourer here at Mérivel and he has also announced himself as the "estate physician". He delivered a baby yesterday, a little girl to one of the kitchen staff. There was much celebration. Later, I helped Robert clean out the stables. It was really hard work and smelly, but fun. Afterwards, I collected vegetables from the walled garden: onions, garlic, a large red pepper, two lemons. I am learning to cook some of our meals. Michel the Bean says we can take anything we fancy from the land for our food. Robert's parents agreed. Claudette and her family are organizing their departure for Paris. Why don't you stay here? I begged her. I hate to see her go.

14 September 1940

Claudette's parents are not taking her with them to Paris. She is going to be enrolled at the *lycée* in Nice where I am studying. Hooray!!!

16 October 1940

I cannot picture the scene, but a wall topped with yards and yards of curled barbed wire has been constructed all around the neighbourhood where we lived in Warsaw. These enclosed districts are for Jews and are called the "small ghetto" and the "big ghetto". I heard in the baker's this morning, the *boulangerie* at the end of the local village street, that the entire walled area is under surveillance and patrolled by armed German guards. Only Jews and a few gypsies are inhabiting these imprisoned zones where the residents are no longer given any freedom of movement. They cannot leave without permission and that is almost impossible to attain.

This is hearsay, I am reporting, words spoken by other refugees we meet about the place or locals at the baker's or wherever. Who knows what is true any longer? Any news that does get through to us, usually via other refugees from Warsaw or elsewhere, sounds so frightening, but it is impossible to know what is actually happening back at home. Home. Our little pink house. It seems such a distant memory and a place that I am not connected to at all.

We can only pray for everyone's safety. Whenever we meet other Polish refugees we pool whatever news we have heard in the hope that at some point, we ourselves will learn something about the health and wellbeing of our own family members. It is very upsetting. I have never felt so isolated and yet I love it where we are now and that makes me feel guilty. Do we have the right to be free when neighbours and other ordinary people like us, from the very same street where we used to live, are living as prisoners?

Could the same thing happen here in France now that the Germans are in charge? Not here in our Free Zone, of course. We are safe, but elsewhere in France. Is Uncle Adam safe? Does being married to Lidia offer him protection? I have no idea.

Father and the doctor are next door with Mama. She is getting weaker every day and is being fed only liquid foods. She hasn't been out of bed for over a week.

17 October 1940

I am reaching the last page of this diary so am writing in small squiggly letters to fit in all my thoughts…

A new law has been passed, permitting local prefects – they are like policemen or sheriffs, I think – to intern Jewish foreigners. That means us. We could be locked up. It seems that living in France is no longer safe. The "Statute on Jews" is the name of the law.

Mama is terribly weak and does not even want the soup that I made for her.

20 October 1940

Mama, my wonderful *Matkować,* died early this morning. Papa was with her, holding her hand. There were tears in his eyes when he called me in to stroke her face and say goodbye to her. He was shuffling like an old man. "My Ruby," he whispered.

I cannot believe it. My mother has gone. Why, oh why?

21 October 1940

As is the Jewish tradition, Mama's burial will not be delayed. However, we are not going to the synagogue in Nice. Mama will go into a Christian grave because it would not be safe for us to advertise ourselves publicly. "Better she lies in rest in the company of friends," said Papa. We are not in danger here, but there are informers even in this region. Mama is to be buried in the grounds of Mérivel close to the chapel. So, as long as we live in this vicinity she will always be close to us. Should we ever return to Poland, Father will have her remains exhumed and we will take her home. For now she can be at peace in this wonderful place.

I have reached the last blank page in my diary; my tears are smudging the ink and the letters are spreading, so I'd better finish. In any case, I have nothing more to say except that I thought, after everything, all the hardships we have endured, we would be secure, that our lives could begin to know happiness again, but it has not turned out that way. I have lost someone so precious to me. I cannot quite grasp it, I cannot comprehend that this separation will be forever.

Life is cruel and horrid.

The End

New York, 1948

Continued...

Dearest Claudette,

After Mama died, I gave up my diary for almost two years. I was not capable of sharing my thoughts even with myself. Grasping the reality of our lives was too complex, too challenging. Everything became fragmented and yet on the surface there were so many good things. You were a major part of them and your parents' generosity almost certainly saved our lives.

The second book enclosed with these letters is, as it were, Book Two, but before you read on, because you might be surprised by the big gap in time, I wanted to remind you of that year, that period of time, late into 1940 and onwards. The loss of my mother coincided with your parents' decision to keep you at Mérivel instead of educating you in Paris. I don't know what you felt about their decision, but I was really excited. Robert Fournier, the estate manager's son, was fun and kind to me, but you were the one I loved; you were the one I judged my friend and you seemed to feel the same way even as early on as that autumn and winter when I was so lonely, so bereft.

Do you remember how we started to go riding together? You were very patient with me when I kept wobbling about, falling off, feet slipping from the stirrups, while trying not to be afraid. You never went galloping on ahead as I knew you so easily could. And then came Bess, the pony you and your parents gave me that Christmas of 1940. I couldn't believe my eyes when you led me blindfolded into the stables and there, when you untied the hankie from my face, there she was, Bess. She was so beautiful. What happened to her? Do you still have her there at the farm? Honey-toned Bess. She was the first, the only, pet I had ever owned. Here, in New York, we live in an apartment, but we have a gorgeous white Persian cat. Father wasn't too happy about the idea at first, but I was determined. I wanted a creature living with us so that we weren't able to just pack up and leave and give up our lives again. When we first arrived, owning a cat helped me to be secure. It gave me the feeling that Papa and I have finally made ourselves a permanent home. If only my dear Matkować could have made it to the States with us. We still miss her so very much, and the sadness is that we have no photographs. Every last thing that we owned was lost or stolen or sold to buy us food or bribe somebody along the way, to help us travel one step further along our road to freedom.

You must be asking about Marek and Aunt Irina. I can almost hear the questions all the way across the Atlantic Ocean, but I will answer them later. Now, you must be patient, please. Let me return to your lovely Mérivel and that brutal end for us to 1940 and the following spring of 1941.

Mama was gone. Our family was split in two. Father had no employment except at Mérivel and yet, though my heart was bursting with so much sorrow, on the surface I was having a really good life. I was doing well at the lycée. Every day was a discovery, every day brought new reasons to want to continue to live. I will be forever grateful to you and Robert, but especially you, for giving me that energy, that determination not to give in to my sorrows.

I don't remember too much about 1941 without a diary to remind me of the details, but let me recall what I can. It was a very harsh winter in Paris, violent blizzards rent the occupied city, German soldiers frequented every café, every restaurant, your parents wrote to you, and petrol rationing was brought in. Taxis were powered by men on bicycles in spite of the cruel weather conditions, but we were south and we were warm.

"If we were still in Paris," you grinned, eyes sparkling as you read me the news from your letter, "we could bury ourselves in the Café de Flore and drink cups and

cups *of* chocolat chaud *and make faces at the horrid Germans. Remember what fun we had, Rebecca? Oh, how I miss Paris. It can be so dull here.*"

I was hurt by those words. I was not enough for you, it seemed. How vulnerable I was!

I turned fourteen that year and my body was changing and developing, and my mother was not there to answer all my questions and help me understand what was happening to me, but you shared your innocent knowledge with me. The stories of the birds and bees, you called them. Les histoires d'amour. I found it all a bit frightening at first.

I remember how startling the seasons were; the way Robert's family worked the land as though they were kneading bread, and the groaning baskets of food they delivered to Father and me. I remember the colours of spring and the palest of blossoms on the almond trees that came so early. February, I think it was, and later how we climbed for the furry green fruits and cracked them open and gobbled them up instantly: tender, milky nuts. I remember learning to cook new vegetables I had never tasted before. I remember eating my first pomegranate, a fruit that means a great deal in the Jewish traditions, but that I had never seen before. I remember the beehives in the lavender gardens behind the main house and Michel the Bean extracting the *combs of honey while I looked on, all wrapped up to protect myself from their stings, just like he told me to. I remember I asked him about the bees' love stories and he burst out laughing at me. I remember father killing a chicken in the yard by wringing its neck and then we had to cook it and eat it and I couldn't swallow a mouthful because I feared it would turn on the plate and come back to life. I remember you and Robert giving me my first sip of wine (produced at Mérivel) and you being amazed that I had never tasted wine before. Above all, I remember seeing Robert kiss you in the stable courtyard after you had both returned from a whole afternoon out riding together and you were looking flushed and so full of life. I had not intended to spy. I was just there, combing Bess, talking to her, and you didn't see me. You seemed to be so completely wrapped up in one another. I felt so jealous, so hurt and betrayed as though I was being locked out, as though you shared a secret liking between you that I could never be a part of. I cried so hard that night because I was alone and because Mérivel was your home and Robert's family's home and he was a native of the region and I was an intruder. I was someone, along with my father, who was being shown kindness. We did not belong. We did not belong anywhere. Once I began to get swallowed up in those sorrows, the loss*

I liked him so much, but part of me was glad that he was gone, relieved, because I had you all to myself again.

Do you remember how we all celebrated when America joined the war? It was that winter after Robert had left for the mountains, 8 December 1941, a little over a year after Mama died. There had been a horrible bombing somewhere I had never heard of (it was Pearl Harbour) and that decided Mr Roosevelt, the American president, to commit to our plight fully. Everyone thought it would be the end of the war very shortly, that Hitler would be arrested and punished and we could all get on with our lives. The mood that Christmas was upbeat and positive. Your parents invited us for a few days up into the mountains, to the very village that, little did we know it, would become our next home, our next place of refuge: Saint-Martin-Vésubie. We stayed with you all in a hotel. I think your father was doing everything he could to make our lives acceptable, but there was still a very long way to go before that could be achieved.

I had already turned fifteen by the time I considered my diary again…

The Diary of Rebecca Mortkowicz
Book 2

1942

24 July 1942

It is summer. School has finished now for quite a few weeks and, because I have my days free, I have decided to begin another diary. A new book. Crisp fresh pages. No ink stains, no scruffy bent corners. Pristine emptiness. I wonder what the stories will be that will turn these pages into chapters of my life? I am determined that there will be more joyful memories to write about than the last pages of my first book.

26 July 1942

It is very hot and I cannot take Bess out in the midday sun so I get up really early, when Father rises, and I ride with her then. I have grown more confident and we go off the estate together towards the mountains, the lower Alps, where it is a little cooler and where I feel as though I have nature to myself. I love to watch the sun as it rises up from behind the craggy hills and creeps towards the sea. Bess grazes while I sit cross-legged on the crumbly earth, munching my breakfast of fruit, local bread – baked in the early hours and warm when I collect it from the kitchens – cheese and a container of milk, inhaling the perfumes of the plants. The plants are known as the *garrigue*, the mountain flora of the Mediterranean. They smell absolutely delicious, and it is possible to cook with many of them, using them to add flavour and spice to all our dishes. Mama would have enjoyed these herbs for her fine cooking. Oh, Mama. The loss of her does not seem to get any easier, and I know *Tata* feels the same. In fact, it is worse for him and I have to remind myself not to moan or walk about like an object of doom and gloom.

Today is Marek's birthday. He turns six today. I close my eyes and try to picture what he must look like now. How sad he would be if he learned that his mother, whom he hardly knew, has departed and left us all…

2 August 1942

News has reached us from Uncle Adam that the French police have arrested thousands of Jews and they are being held as prisoners in Paris at a sports centre called the Winter Velodrome. What does this mean? I thought we were beginning to win the war. Uncle Adam also wrote to Father that he and Aunt Lidia are intending to take a promenade. Promenade means going for a walk. I was puzzled. *Tata* says that Uncle is informing him in a kind of code that they are leaving the city. Obviously, they did not say where they are headed. They are the last thread of contact with our family. We are cut off now, all is severed.

I thought all this fear was gone from our lives. The fear of being hunted and punished for nothing except who we are and what we believe, and we are not even an orthodox family. It does not make any sense to me.

4 August 1942

Claudette and I went to Nice to meet with friends of hers. We sat in a café and guzzled fresh lemonade and then she and I strolled along the front, the *Baie des Anges*, or Angels Bay in English, and watched the tourists. The sea was almost turquoise and as smooth as a sheet of glass. Everywhere was so quiet. Claudette told me that before the war people used to come here by the thousands, pouring out of trains from Paris and London and other cities in northern Europe, even as far away as Russia, to spend their holidays relaxing on the beaches, playing ball games and tanning their skin. She said that this strip of beach, known as the French Riviera or Côte d'Azur, was very fashionable before the war. There are certainly many elegant hotels in this city, built for this very purpose. The poshest of them all is the Negresco, which was used as a hospital during the previous European war (the one my father calls the Great War).

As we walked by the sea, looking across the wide avenue to the grand hotels and villas, Claudette pointed out a splendid mansion set back behind tropical gardens with tall palm trees. The house was not as grand or as extensive as Mérivel but still it looked like something out of a dream. "A friend of my father's is staying there," she said to me.

I didn't think anything about it until she added, "I think your father knows him too." This piqued my curiosity.

"Who is he?" I asked.

"A German writer and journalist, Theodor Wolff. He came down here to escape Hitler long before the war began. Father says he is brilliant and that he was very famous and influential in Germany, but the situation is difficult for him now."

I was not sure what Claudette meant by that remark. Isn't the war difficult for everyone? Nice has changed even since we first arrived here. The taxis are horse-drawn carriages now because there is petrol rationing. At the newsstands, the headlines suggest that the Allies – that is

126

Britain, America, France and a few other countries, like Australia – are doing really well and are beginning to push Hitler back, but that does not seem to fit in with the arrest-of-Jews stories we have been hearing. Father gets very nervous when I go anywhere alone. He worries that I will not be safe, that I might be forcibly taken. "There are those who know we are Jewish," he warns me, "and there are some who might inform the wrong people out of malice or for their own gain." He rarely leaves the estate. He holds regular clinics at Mérivel where local people, mainly pregnant mothers or those with small children come to visit him. Otherwise he labours with Monsieur and Madame Fournier, who worry about their son's safety. The tractors and machinery have been stored and the essential work is carried out manually with horses to pull the old machinery. Machinery that does not require petrol.

5 August 1942

Claudette accompanied me on my ride with Bess this morning. We took a route inland that was so beautiful. There were vineyards everywhere, each full of ripening grapes, and we stopped to walk Belle and Bess when the going got too hot or the ground was too rough. She told me that Robert's parents had received a message from him. Henri, the son of Jean, the plumber, who lives in the village next to Mérivel is also in the Résistance with Robert. The news is that Henri and Robert are both safe, living rough, sleeping under the stars somewhere in the mountains, but doing their best to help free France and expel the Germans. I wondered if Claudette ever dreamed about the time he kissed her.

"Do you miss him?" I asked her. She shrugged. "Sometimes," she admitted eventually. He was rather like a brother to her, she explained, because they had grown up together.

He hadn't kissed her like a brother.

I asked her to tell me all about the Résistance and what they are doing in the mountains, and her reply was that it was best not to speak about it.

"Why are you so secretive?" I burst out laughing because we were miles from anywhere sitting at the foot of a hill in a scrubby field, munching on sticky-sweet peaches we had picked from one of the trees before we set out. "There's no one listening, silly!"

Claudette says that those who have disappeared to join the Résistance are mostly younger citizens and they are very brave but are in great danger. Many French people even disagree with what they are up to and will report them to the police if they get the opportunity. If they are captured, they are taken before firing squads and shot.

"It's rather like the Jewish Problem, we should never speak publicly about our thoughts and feelings on this subject or what we know about these matters. It is dangerous."

I was silenced by this remark. The Jewish Problem, what could Claudette mean?

I asked Father later what he knew about the Jewish Problem. He told me that in Germany in 1939, the Nazis – they are the Germans working for Hitler – had drawn up a paper of how best to get rid of Jews, "which is why so many of us have moved from our homelands," he explained. "But of course, little robin, we do not go away so easily. The Germans cannot make Jews disappear. They cannot simply exterminate us, but they can make our lives very uncomfortable, which is what they have been doing and why we have moved home so frequently. Fortunately, there are some very fine people in this world, like Mr Lautrec, Claudette's father, who wants to help us. He is a man who should be honoured for what he does because it is not without risk. Look how he has looked after us and there are others living along the coast here that he feeds and supports in various ways."

"Is Theodor Wolff also helped by Mr Lautrec?" I asked. Father was surprised by my question.

"How do you know of him, little robin?"

"Claudette pointed out the huge house he lives in."

"He is being lodged there, yes. He was a very outspoken journalist in Germany who spoke out against many cruelties in his homeland and who saw what Hitler intended at an early stage. If he had stayed in Germany he would have been imprisoned or executed."

Over dinner *Tata* told me all about the French Résistance who are aiding the Allies. They pass on information to British Intelligence. This helps the British plan their war moves, their strategies. They hide British soldiers and secret agents and they assist them to escape if they are at risk of being captured. The work of the Résistance is varied. They are led or guided by an important French soldier who is in exile in London. His name is General Charles de Gaulle. He sends messages over the wireless encouraging France not to give in to the German occupation and to fight on. All these groups, these volunteers who are in hiding, are jointly known as the Résistance because they are resisting the Occupation.

Last year, Father told me, all communists here in France joined forces to support the Résistance movement and that has made them much more powerful.

I lay awake thinking about all that I had learned. How exciting it must be to join the Résistance. When I am older if the War is not over, then I will go and hide in the mountains and work with them. I wondered if I might bump into Robert and sleep under the stars alongside him. Would he kiss me too?

3 September 1942

Claudette and I hennaed my hair today. One of the women who works in the kitchens, Anissa, is a Tunisian, and she has henna powder posted to her from North Africa. Once the powder has been mixed with water and turned into a gungy paste, it is amazing what she does with it – she decorates her ankles. It looks as though she is wearing bracelets or swirly cuffs of snakes, rose petals and curled leaves. The decorations are lovely, but the henna hasn't worked on my hair. I look really strange as though I have plonked a bright orange brush on my head. All Claudette said was I look more French now. I don't agree at all. No French girl I have ever seen looks like this. Just weird. When I went back to the cottage *Tata* asked, "What on earth have you done to yourself, little robin?" I told him it was a disguise to keep me safe from the Nazis. He smiled but he didn't laugh. I haven't noticed before but his hair is going grey. He looks much older. Maybe I should suggest to him that he asks Anissa to do his hair too or even design his bald patch with henna!

I agreed that my hair looks silly, but then I told him

about how Anissa decorates herself with painted ankle bands and that Claudette suggested we do the same.

"I forbid it, robin, do you hear me!" He rounded on me with a force I have rarely seen before. It quite startled me.

"Nothing that can identify you, or single you out, do you understand?"

He spoke with a very serious voice, but more quietly, almost gravely, and then he picked up his newspaper and a glass of wine and stepped out onto the terrace.

12 November 1942

British and American troops have landed in Algeria in North Africa, which is French territory. Everyone seems quite triumphant about it but I am not quite sure why. The war is here not over there.

16 November 1942

HELP! The German soldiers are moving out of the occupied areas of France and infiltrating the Free Zone. Their intention now is to control ALL of France. Father heard that they marched into Montpelier two or three days ago. So he was right. If we had stayed there, we would be hunted out now, rounded up and captured.

I am not quite sure exactly what is going on but it seems that the British and Americans along with troops from other friendly nations, the Allies, are moving closer to France and this is a threat to the Germans stationed here. The Allies are intending or will attempt to reconquer the occupied territories. Hitler (no one calls him mister anymore – he is way too nasty) is retaliating by spreading his troops into the areas that were never his.

Will it be safe to remain here near Nice? It is a question that everyone is asking themselves.

Italians soldiers have started to arrive, pouring across the border, descending from the Alps, which also range into Italy. They are here to guard this stretch of coast and are known as the Italian Fourth Army. Everyone is a little afraid because they are on Hitler's side. We have packed up a few belongings and could be forced to flee again at any moment. I wondered about that writer in Nice. Will he have to go too? When I asked Papa, he told me that there are thousands of Jews in hiding in this corner of France because it had been judged a secure place. If the Germans reach this corner, we will all be in danger.

I cannot understand why the Nazi Germans cannot forget about the "Jewish Problem" and just get on with their lives. We are not doing them any harm. We are just trying to live our lives like everybody else. What's their difficulty?

2 December 1942

A teenage boy turned up at the estate this morning enquiring after work. He looked ever so bedraggled. His name, he said, is Léon but I am not sure. Michel the Bean took him in and found him somewhere to sleep in one of the barns and sent him off to the kitchens for a solid breakfast. He looked pretty tired and hungry. *Tata* says he is Jewish and that perhaps he has been separated from his family. We must be very kind to him.

3 December 1942

I was up before light and walked slowly across to the stables, listening to the dawn chorus. Even in this season, the birds make a fair racket. The winter sun was still low in the sky when I took Bess out. We did not go all that far. After, while I was brushing her down and cleaning out her box, Léon put his head round the door. He offered to help me, but seemed a bit awkward, explaining that Mr Bean had sent him. I gave him a rake and told him to gather the horse muck into piles and wheel it round to Mr Bean who uses it as manure on the land. It's a smelly job and I don't like doing it. I tried to engage Léon in conversation about where he'd come from but he was very reticent. I don't think he wanted to be in the stables at all. I felt sorry for him. He's quite handsome now that he has had a good wash, but he looks ever so unhappy.

4 December 1942

Anissa cut my hair yesterday. I couldn't bear the orange any longer so we have chopped it really short and now instead of looking like a garden broom, I look like a boy.

5 December 1942

We have all been invited for Christmas supper up at the main house with Claudette's family on the evening of the 24th. I am so excited. Her grandparents have arrived already. Claudette's father said that it is to a be a Mérivel celebration and whatever our religious beliefs he would like everyone to attend. Anissa is a Muslim, she told me yesterday, and has never participated in a Christian celebration before. I told her that there will be a tree and it will be decorated and then lit up and Christians keep presents under the tree and that their leader was a Jew. Claudette couldn't explain what the significance of the tree is, but she confirmed that there will be presents.

I am really looking forward to it. I wish I had money to buy some gifts but I haven't got anything at all. After the holidays, I might see if I can find myself some temporary work.

8 December 1942

The city of Nice is full of Italians. There are soldiers everywhere but they appear to be kind and, thank heavens, don't ask for identity papers. They seem more concerned about the celebrations for Christmas than the war. There were groups of them standing outside several of the bars down along the seafront drinking and smoking. They wave and say *Bonjour Madamoiselle* with very funny accents that make Claudette and me giggle. The soldiers seem very attracted to her with her tall figure and long wavy hair. One fellow actually stopped us and asked her her name, then invited her for a *café,* but she didn't accept. He was very good looking though. I felt a bit piqued that he did not invite me to join them.

16 December 1942

Hooray! No more school till next year!

Léon confided this afternoon that he has lost his family. They were taken from their apartment way over the other side of France near Toulouse in August and he has no idea where they have gone. He is Jewish, not that he acknowledged it but I gleaned it from all that he said. When I asked him why he hadn't been with his parents and younger brother, he said that he had been sent away to a school, or rather an institution where you live in and work. It was when he went home for a weekend, he discovered his family had gone. He walked through the front door, which had been left ajar, and the first thing he spotted was a gilded vase his mother had brought with her from Berlin in pieces on the wooden floor. Penetrating further, he found a fox wrap lying in the bath and broken perfume bottles. His father's reading glasses, distorted and smashed, were behind the bedroom door, trodden underfoot judging by the state of them. He stayed one night there alone, waiting for his family's return but nobody appeared, and there was no food in the house. He was hungry and terrified.

It was the old neighbour with filmy eyes who knocked on the second day and found him huddled in a corner in the empty apartment. The old man tipped him off. He told Léon to disappear from there as fast as he could and never to return. "You are not safe," the neighbour warned him. "The French police are looking for the likes of you." Poor Léon has been on the run ever since, moving further east, not daring to stop for more than a night, not even to look for or enquire after his family. He has kept moving, as we did before we arrived here. He's seventeen and whispered that he's scared he'll never see his parents again and what will he do? I promised he could stay with us if we had to go anywhere again and that we would say he is my brother, but given that we are Jewish, he is not going to be very safe with us. Still, at least he can pretend he has a family. Lord, it was horrible, horrible losing Mama, but what if I came home and found that *Tata* was also gone and I was all alone in the world? I cannot imagine anything more dreadful. All alone in the world in a foreign country. How terrifying. I will be especially kind to Léon. Actually, that is not difficult because he is really nice.

18 December 1942

This afternoon, while we were digging up potatoes together, I confided to Léon that I am Jewish. He burst out laughing, threw down his spade and hugged me tightly, which made me blush and come over all embarrassed. "I know that, silly," he whispered into my hair. His hands were covered in earth and felt rough against my skin as he stroked my cheek, but I didn't mind.

19 December 1942

It has been decreed that all Jews living in France must now receive a stamp on their identity papers. This is to distinguish us from the others, as Jews. "*Un Juif*". But we have no papers. Father said that even if we did possess any, he would not take our documents to be stamped. "If I did, they would know about us; we would be on their lists. No, little robin, we are better to keep a low profile and remain outside the system now. It will make our escape easier."

Our escape? My heart sank. I thought we had finally settled, finally found a home for ourselves.

25 December 1942

Christmas supper last night was amazing. Everybody received a gift. Everybody. We sang French songs round the grand piano and we ate a groaning great meal with three sizzling, roasted geese served as the main course. A choice of wine – red, white or the local rosé – was poured generously into everyone's glasses no matter their age or status. Even Anissa, who is a Muslim and is not allowed to drink alcohol, was offered a tiny sip. Monsieur and Madame Lautrec created an atmosphere that made everyone feel as though they belong here and are part of this big farm family. I wish there was some way in which I could show my appreciation for everything they are doing for us.

My gift was a fountain pen. Léon also received one – his is black and mine burgundy red – while Father was given a very splendid small leather suitcase. He smiled quietly when he received it and just kept nodding. I feared he was thinking that we might be packing it before too long. Anissa's gift, when she shyly opened it, was a beautiful woven shawl.

At midnight, a local priest who had also dined with us, a man the Lautrecs referred to as "Father" though I don't believe he is related to them, celebrated a service in the estate chapel, just near where Mama is buried. They called it Midnight Mass. It was in Latin so I could not understand what was happening at all, but there were many candles and bells ringing and there was smoke from burning incense which smelled quite powerful. I felt quite dizzied by it all.

It reminded me of the Christmas Day when Aunt Lidia and I went to the cathedral at Notre Dame. I wonder where she and Uncle Adam are now. I do so hope they are safe.

1943

30 January 1943

There have been raids on Jewish families in Marseille, which is about two hours west along the coast from here. A door-to-door city search took place, checking papers, and then the Round-up, as it is being called, was centred in Marseille's old port. People were beaten and hurt. Almost 2,000 Jews were arrested and taken away. We don't know to where. What is even more horrible about this news is that the French police seemed to be aiding the Nazis in this rounding-up of entire families.

February 1943

We are not safe here any more, and we are being encouraged to move inland, higher into the mountains, but remaining close to the Italian border because these are the areas where the Italians are in charge and the Italians don't hate Jews and they don't put us on trains and send us to goodness knows where.

I cannot bear the thought of leaving Mérivel, leaving Bess and leaving Claudette. This afternoon when I thought I was alone in the stable, Claudette found me crying like a baby into Bess's mane. "I don't want to go away again," I sobbed. "What about Mama? We cannot leave Mama."

"You'll be back very soon," my friend assured me. "It's less than two hours' drive from here and I will come up and visit you as frequently as I can."

"What about Léon?"

"Father says he must go with you."

I was pleased that Mr Lautrec was also encouraging Léon to come with us. But why must we leave this wonderful place?

7 March 1943 The old port at Nice

Father and I, along with Léon, have been loaded into a bus alongside two dozen other Jewish refugees including a very old rabbi who seems barely able to walk. Poor old fellow, covered in blankets, as weak and beaten by life as Mama was before she died. Only a handful of our travelling companions are Polish. The others have fled from Germany, some from Austria, a couple from Belgium, but together we boarded the rather decrepit coach parked in the harbour of Nice. There were three other buses, also waiting to be filled. Each driver waited patiently, smoking cigarettes, getting out of his cab when he got restless, exchanging opinions with one or other of his colleagues, glancing at his watch, waiting to be on his way to transport us inland. The information we have is that we are being taken to a village high in the mountains where we can live without fear, where the Nazis will not find us. But haven't we been told that same story before? Isn't that what we were promised here? How long can we keep running?

I am heartbroken to leave the sea. I have loved my life here in Nice.

The faces on the bus. What a library of emotions on quiet display. Although it is not cold – I can feel spring in the air and the sun is shining across the bay, glinting and dancing on the water – several of the women are muffled up in heavy coats with scarves tied round their heads. Their eyes are puffy and sad-looking.

Finally, I spied Léon and waved frantically to him but he was boarded into one of the other buses. He acknowledged my call as he stepped out of sight. I do so hope we won't be separated.

20 March 1943 Saint-Martin-Vésubie

I have had so little time to write, but I don't want to forget, to lose, these precious alpine memories.

Here is what I recall of our journey, of our arrival up here in this small town, little more than a sprawling village in the mountains. As our old bus ascended, the day was sharp and clear and the views sweeping down to the sea were very dramatic. The cranky old coach climbed for almost three hours without stopping. Our journey was more than sixty kilometres along winding, bumpy roads sometimes no wider than goat tracks. It grew colder as we chugged higher, spiralling into the interior. We passed through a gorge, a deep ravine with high limestone walls on either side of us. The sheer height of the rock-face kept this passage hidden from the sun and made it quite spooky. There was a woman on her own who was seated just behind me. She had a tattered scarf of many faded colours knotted around her head. She was about the same age as *Matkować* would have been. I noticed her properly when she began making sobbing or heaving sounds as though she could not catch her breath. I turned to see if she was unwell and her whole body was shaking, really shaking. I don't know if she was afraid in that dark ravine or cold. Father took off his overcoat and passed it back to her. Take this, he whispered, but she shook her head. He insisted and then knelt up on his seat and wrapped the garment round her shoulders. She stopped resisting; her shaking subsided a little and eventually she closed her eyes. A shadow of a smile broke across her face. It was like a silent thank you to my father for taking care of her. I couldn't stop looking at her as she slept with her head lolling back against the seat. Suddenly, it was as though she was my mother.

"Open your eyes and look at the view, *Matka*," I wanted to whisper to her. (We were beyond the ravine by this point.) "Those are chestnut trees. See the rivers. Look at the water plunging way below us. Please, Mama, I beg you not to give in. Look, look, there's a man wearing a navy-blue beret, riding a donkey with a switch of olive branches attached to the donkey's haunches. Please, please be excited that we are still safe and we're travelling to a new life," but the woman half-buried beneath *Tata's* coat was not my mother and she continued to sleep, not bothering to pay attention to where we were going. I sighed and returned my gaze to beyond the windows in time to catch the farmer on the donkey disappear out of sight behind a rock.

A little later and quite suddenly, looming high above us, as though in a fairy tale, growing out of the cleft of the mountain, I caught sight of a stone village – it looked as though it was clinging for its life to the rocks, fastened by boot strings – and my mind rushed forward to the future, to where we were going to live now and all that lay ahead for us. 930 metres above sea level, surrounded by conifer forests, sat Saint-Martin-Vésubie. The village that was to be our home, our new safe haven. For a few moments I was excited and then everything and everyone we were leaving behind came crowding in on me and I felt a sinking sense in my stomach. Why should this be any better, any safer? As soon as we settle here and make friends, might we be forced to up sticks again and tramp on to somewhere else? Will we live like this for the rest of our lives? When will we understand that there is no place left, no place safe for us to run to?

It was the middle of the afternoon when we eventually stepped out of the coach. Troops of Italian soldiers and carabinieri awaited us and we had to line up and give them our names and then they allocated us a place to spend the night. Léon's bus arrived almost an hour after ours but we managed to persuade the Italian captain that he was with us and that we did not wish to be separated again. The dark-haired man smiled and agreed; we were very fortunate.

There was an easy-going mood about the place. No sense of threat. Many languages were being spoken. No one was afraid to speak his mother tongue. There was no necessity to hide from where he came.

We are free, I thought. At last, we are free.

21 March 1943

We spent our first night in Saint-Martin-Vésubie close to the town's central square at the Châtaigneraie Hotel where dozens of beds had been made ready in the restaurant area. On our second day, Father found us an apartment on the ground floor of the most elegant, turn-of-the-century house. It has a very large garden with an iron swing. The rooms are spacious with tall ceilings. Father and I have bedrooms of our own while Léon sleeps in the living room on a sofa. Upstairs, another family with three small children is in residence, two boys and a girl. They are also Jewish, from Hungary. *Tata* exchanged a few words with the man this morning in Yiddish. Their name is Levitt. Mr Levitt said that they had been here for almost two months, having fled from south-western France. He is a pianist by profession, but has not been able to practise or play for over two years. Instead, he spends his time composing music. Father said he would try to find someone in the village who might be kind enough to loan us a piano. Then he will ask Mr Levitt to give me lessons. I would enjoy that very much. It made me think about Aunt Lidia. She would like it here. She could give concerts and everybody would listen to her music in awe and then applaud her loudly. I miss her and Uncle Adam.

On our second evening, after we had moved into our house, or perhaps I should say installed the few bits of clothing, photographs, memorabilia we are still in possession of, I strolled to the centre of the village flanked by Father and Léon. There, we shopped for food to prepare in our own kitchen where we have a big stove made of cast iron. It heats food and water and will keep the house warm. Together, we walked downhill to the central square where I caught sight of the woman who had been sitting behind us on the bus, the one who reminded me of *Matka*. She was alone, hunched on a bench, crying.

"Is she ill, should we go to her?" I asked Papa.

"She's tired. Quite possibly she has lost someone. I think it better to leave her to her sorrow in peace. This mountain air will do her spirits the world of good."

"Perhaps she has lost everyone, like me," added Léon.

"You haven't lost us," I whispered to him.

1 April 1943

There is the most wonderful sound and a curious sight here. Water flows through the streets. I have never seen such a spectacle before. It is a stream flowing fast, descending within narrow, man-made gullies cut into the centre of the deeply sloping cobbled streets and alleyways. It is because we are in the mountains, I was told by a sales lady in one of the shops, a dusty *papeterie* where I can buy paper and pencils and all kinds of bits of stationery – if only I were able to write letters to all our loved ones, but I have no addresses for anyone.

The sales lady told me that in the winter the mountains are covered in thick layers of snow but when spring comes and the sun melts the snow, it flows fast through the perched, slanting town.

3 April 1943

You can stand in the centre of this little town and enjoy spectacular views down into the valley of Vésubie or crane your head and look upwards and gaze at mountain peaks soaring heavenwards. It would be very difficult to find anywhere more natural and beautiful. I take such pleasure strolling here, there and everywhere, investigating the narrow lanes, turning a corner and there before me is a panoramic view. And I am free, that is what makes the nature and the clear clean air all the more delicious. We have found freedom.

6 April 1943

The local people speak French with a very thick accent and it is difficult for me to understand them. I will get used to it though, for sure. In the time that we have been in France, I have easily learned the language and I am really very fluent now, but here I have difficulties. The accent is twangy and strange, twangier than Michel the Bean's. Here, the vocabulary is a mixture of Italian and French, a dialect from a region in Italy just over the border known as Piedmont. This is why the locals can communicate so easily with the Italian soldiers. I read in the village library that this part of France was ruled by Italy until 1860.

7 April 1943

Léon and I have been enrolled in one of the local schools. He is two classes above me but we can walk there together and if he is studying later, I can work in the library and wait for him. It really is like having a brother, a real brother. I haven't thought about Marek in so long. Father and I rarely talk about Poland now. He does not even talk about Mama all that frequently. I think he prefers to remember her by himself. He sleeps with their wedding photograph by his bed.

10 April 1943

Mr Levitt, our upstairs neighbour, has nicknamed me Rivka. He says that is how my name would be spoken if I had been born in Budapest. Budapest is the capital of Hungary and it was where the Levitt family lived before they left their homeland in 1940. Unlike Poland, he told me, the Jews were less threatened in Hungary, but he preferred to take his family out of their country because you could never be sure with Hitler. Hungary was a trading partner of both Nazi Germany and Fascist Italy. Even so, Hitler hates Jews and hunts them wherever he can find them, so it is better to be clear of his clutches.

12 April 1943

We shop at market stalls and buy fresh sheep and goat cheeses and fill our baskets with locally-grown vegetables. Léon has begged seeds from one or two of the farmers and intends to plant up a vegetable patch in our back garden behind the swing. There is plenty of space. He told me he learnt basic farming skills when he and his family were living over on the west side of France. Digging gardens was how he earned his pocket money.

16 April 1943

In the square last night, the principal *place*, where people meet to chat and gossip and sit at cafés drinking coffee or beer, passing the time of day, there were almost as many Italians as French. The Italians are in charge here but now the dominant influx is us, the Jews. Before we all arrived here, the French inhabitants numbered a little more than one thousand and now the population is over 3,000 counting all refugees and soldiers. It must be very strange for these isolated mountain people with their funny accents who are mostly kind to us even if sometimes they charge us extortionate prices (Father says) for lodgings and foodstuffs. Do they feel overrun by all us foreigners?

One toothless old hag said to Léon yesterday when he argued the price of a pail of milk, "You're a Jew, you have money and gold aplenty. You can afford to pay, whereas we are mountain folk, we are peasants with nothing but our hands to dig the earth with. We won't turn you in, but you must pay us for the privilege."

Do all the villagers think like this woman or is she the exception? I hope she is.

24 April 1943

Another thing I really like about Saint-Martin is that there are dozens of fountains here. The falling water sounds like chimes in the air. Behind the town, mountain peaks soar skywards. These are the Alps. In winter, they are covered in snow, but now they are green and so attractive. Many of the local townspeople graze their sheep up there. I am looking forward to going on long hikes and discovering the countryside. I hope Léon will come with me.

Father and Mr Levitt have decided to start up a chess club.

22 May 1943

Yesterday evening Claudette and her parents drove up here (in a rather swanky open top car) to visit us for a long weekend and to celebrate my birthday. They are staying at the Victoria Hotel, one of the grander establishments, but we have been spending all our time together. It's such fun. Before the war, Claudette told me, this town was a summer resort. Many British tourists came here as well as wealthy families from Paris who found the immense heat down at the coast too much to bear. (I love it!) Due to the altitude, even at the height of summer it is cooler here.

I had been wondering who owned all these elegant villas and why there could be so many available for rental. Since the war began, the tourists have not been coming here so, in a way, the arrival of the Italian soldiers and then the Jews must be helping the local economy. The villa that Papa, Léon and I and the Levitt family are living in belongs to a British couple. Claudette said that her parents know them, but have not seen them for some time because they returned to London in 1939. Their summer house, our present home, has been standing empty for over three years.

It was through Mr Lautrec that we found these lodgings. He gave *Tata* the address. I am very stupid sometimes. It had never occurred to me to ask myself how we can afford our rent. I am certain now that Mr Lautrec is keeping us and Léon. Without him, we would be stranded and without resources.

Claudette and her parents gave me the most amazing birthday present – a very fine gold bracelet. I feel very grown-up with it dangling from my wrist.

30 May 1943

The woman who sat behind us on the bus journey coming from the coast fainted in the main square yesterday evening. She had been shouting at two Italian officers and then she just keeled over. Instead of being angry with her, the two men carried her into their hotel and requested that the proprietor call for a doctor. Léon witnessed the whole scene and he ran for Father.

I saw nothing of all this because I was at the village hall having a piano lesson.

4 June 1943

Mr Levitt is going to give a concert on Saturday 19 June.
I have been hand-designing leaflets and I will nail them to
the trunks of the lovely plane and chestnut trees all around
the squares.

Léon and I went wild-strawberry picking this afternoon.
He is such good company and so knowledgeable about
nature. And I so wanted him to kiss me.

7 June 1943

The weather is so warm that there is talk of bringing the
piano out into the main square and holding the concert
there. There seems to be a great deal of excitement about Mr
Levitt's event. The woman who owns the *papeterie* gave me
half a squire of blank paper for *free* so that I could draw extra
posters. She said that having all of us Jews here has enlivened
village life.

A small temporary synagogue has been set up. We probably won't attend as we are not very religious, but Father says it is refreshing that the townspeople are so tolerant.

The talk in the cafés is always about the war and sometimes about how to escape to Palestine. There are also many questions asked about where the imprisoned Jews are being deported to. No one seems to have any answers. When anyone quizzes the Italians about the subject, they just shrug. "What Hitler does is not our business," one replied. "We don't take orders from him."

13 June 1943

One of the Italian soldiers told Léon that the British have invaded a tiny island off the coast of southern Italy. It is called Pantelleria and is close to Sicily. The Italian confessed that he thinks Hitler's days are numbered and that he personally won't be too sorry because he wants to go home to his family near Milan.

I wish we had a wireless. It is so difficult to find out what is going on up here and so far from the coast.

20 June 1943

What a splendiferous evening we had last night. The air was warm and filled with blossoms and sweet mountain scents. The square was jam-packed with locals, shopkeepers, shepherds, restaurateurs, even two of my school teachers, as well as Italian soldiers and throngs of refugees. From old grannies to toddlers. The grand piano had been set up on a makeshift stage. Mr Levitt, of course, had no evening dress but he looked exceedingly smart with his hair oiled back. He began with Hungarian music, Brahms and Liszt, and the crowd was silent, spellbound. A few standing at the back swayed with delight. Mr Levitt speaks very little French and he was rather shy and apologetic about the fact that he is out of practice because he had not performed in front of an audience in a long time, but people cheered and called out encouraging words in Yiddish and French and he seemed to relax.

Claudette and her parents had driven up for the occasion and Claudette looked ravishing in a pale blue silk frock and white open-toed, small-heeled sandals. She had slung a white fur wrap over her shoulders. One of the hotels, I don't know which one, had set up a long wooden trestle table from which they served iced drinks and snacks. It was like a party. The applause after Mr Levitt had finished resounded throughout the mountains. I could have believed that the animals in the high-altitude forest were listening too. Can Robert hear us having this wonderful party? I asked myself, but I did not say anything about that to Claudette. Afterwards and quite spontaneously, the chairs were all pushed aside and people began to dance. An Italian soldier took over the keyboard and banged out some songs from Naples, very romantic and full of longing. Then another Italian began to sing and a chorus of them broke out. The lady from the stationery shop, who looked very smart in a grey suit, also sang something, a French folk song, I think, because all the French clapped their hands and joined in. It was as though everyone, whoever they were, needed the release of this light-hearted occasion. Léon and Claudette were off dancing with goodness knows who. How Claudette loves to dance, and how everyone queues to dance with her! I felt too shy to put a foot forward until a small, podgy Italian soldier came over to me and held wide his arms, beaming, "Waltz, missus," he cried. "*Per favore, s'il vous plait, bella madamoiselle.*" He swung me about as though I were a broom, walking on my feet, mucking up my summer pumps, but it was fun and he made me laugh until my tummy hurt.

When I looked for Claudette and/or Léon to accompany me back to our villa, I couldn't find either of them and nor could I see them amongst the small crowd remaining, dancing, talking, swaying to unheard music and the night. Father was asleep when I crept in. Léon was not yet home, but I climbed into bed and was asleep in minutes, the music still swirling through my mind.

25 June 1943

Another little girl was born to a Jewish refugee couple this morning. Father presided over the proceedings. It has caused great jubilation within the community. Life, an affirmation of the future. This is the third baby at whose arrival he has assisted. "I am beginning to feel more like a midwife than a paediatrician," he joked at dinner. It was good to see him smile.

3 July 1943

Mr Levitt is quite the town star and he is such a modest man. Still, his concert has created a real sense of community here. It seems to have broken all kinds of barriers and the war has been forgotten just a little bit and the reasons why we are all here together. It is summer. The trees are brilliant green with young leaves. It is impossible to believe that elsewhere people are killing one another, that cruelty such as Hitler's really exists.

I went to buy six fresh eggs this morning and the farmer gave me eight for the same price. "You people are good," he said. "I see kindness amongst you, and you look after each other."

25 July 1943

It is holiday time. Léon, Claudette and I went hiking today. As we climbed – me huffing and puffing – out of Saint-Martin-Vésubie, all the church bells were chiming the Sunday masses. Many of the French residents were to be seen making their way to church. Most of the women, particularly the older women, were dressed entirely in black with lacy veils on their heads. All carried prayer books. I even spotted a few Italian soldiers on their way to the services.

After we grew too tired, struggling up towards the peak of Gelas, we circled back on ourselves and descended to a high-altitude valley where there is a large lake. There, we caught sight of a pair of eagles circling silently overhead. It was wonderful. We were so hot and perspiring profusely from all the marching that we flung off our clothes and dived into the water in our underwear. It was cool, almost cold, sweet water, not salty like the sea. Then we lay in the grass to dry ourselves off, our heads almost spinning from sunlight, heat, bracing water and the altitude. Staring up at the blue sky without a cloud in sight, all around us were mountain peaks. It was perfectly silent, monumental. In the distance, I made out the tinkle of bells. The shepherds hang them from the necks of their grazing flocks of goats and sheep. They call these bells "*picorns*". And then I caught sight of a descending herd of wild dusky brown animals, almost the colour of donkeys but they were taller, with horns, more slender and graceful.

"Oh, look over there!" I cried.

Léon told me to be quiet or they would flee. They were chamois, a kind of cross between a goat and an antelope, and are very shy. Just like Mr Levitt! About a dozen chamois were trooping towards the far extreme of the lake to drink. We sat still as statues watching them. After quenching their thirst, their young played at the water's edge, cavorting with one another for a while on the muddied banks and then the herd just turned as one and wandered away.

The sight of them was such a treat.

I wonder where they are going? I muttered. They moved in a serene fashion as though at peace with their environment and apparently completely unaware of our

168

presence. I suddenly had a picture of what it might be like to live out here, sleeping under the stars, eating berries and wild fruits, never worrying about anything, fearing no enemies, though Léon said some people hunt these lovely creatures.

"Do you think Robert can see us?" I asked Claudette as I rolled over onto my stomach and gazed into her face. She had her eyes closed.

"I doubt he is near here," she mumbled, her red lips barely moving. My eyes were riveted by the freckles on her nose; I was fighting tears. Léon had plucked a stalk of grass and was tickling her neck with it. I felt a sharp pang of jealousy when I saw what he was doing. I could barely look. Everyone loves Claudette. I noticed the way the Italian soldiers watched her when she stepped out of the car in the *place* on Thursday evening. She is so tall and sleek and wears such lovely silk clothes. She told me once that she wants to be an actress when the war is over and she looks like a movie star.

My eyes stung. I sat up sharply, turning away from them both, dragging my knees up to my chest, and concentrated on the shadows of sky and mountains and pine trees in the clear lake. All the images were distorted by my silent crying and the gentle ripples caused by the light breeze. I couldn't see the reflections of my friends because Claudette was lying flat and Léon was raised, leaning on just one elbow.

"Who's older?" I asked. "You, Claudette, or Léon? I think Claudette is. Léon is the baby."

Léon turned his attention towards me and frowned.

"The Germans are coming," replied Claudette very matter-of-fact, without opening her eyes.

"And if they come here and find us, so what? We can't keep running. It's fine for you. You have nothing to worry about."

"They're moving east but it's unlikely they will find you hidden all the way up here. Father says you're safe."

"Well, we have nowhere left to escape to," stated Léon glumly. "So, even if we are not…" He didn't finish his thought but tossed the blade of grass back to the earth.

"Come on, let's swim again." Claudette was on her feet pulling off her blouse before we could voice any objection to another dip before lunch. Léon leapt up after her but I stayed put, arms clenched around my shins, head resting on my knees, watching them as they dived into the water and frolicked together, laughing and splashing one another, both as elegant and athletic as the young chamois. Yes, everyone loves Claudette.

When they finally came out of the water, we ate our picnic of baguette and cheese and then, after picking wild flowers for me and looking for unusual-shaped stones for Léon and one final mad-rush swim for us all, during which Léon caught two enormous trout, we hiked back to the village, singing loudly, listening to our voices echoing back and forth, bouncing off the arena of rocks. Descending through green, green fields, we all held hands. Léon in between us, pulling us onwards when we moaned or felt tired. The fish in his backpack reeked and made us all laugh as we told Léon it was him who smelt. My moment of jealousy had passed. I was just being foolish. In reality I wanted this day to go on forever because I think we all knew, although none of us voiced our premonitions, and even if we had we probably could not have explained the complexities of what we felt, but it was in some way clear to us all, that this happiness, this secure and uncomplicated happiness, could not go on forever.

The reality was that while we were pushing our bodies forward through the cool mountain water, splashing like otters, not so many kilometres away, German soldiers were marching in our direction; tanks were rolling our way. Our perfect lives were under threat.

26 July 1943

I hugged Claudette tightly when we said our "au revoirs", feeling guilty that I had resented her beauty when she is such a good friend to me and I so love my new gold bracelet and I am churned up at every parting from her. Madame Lautrec promised that they will drive up to see us again very soon, before the August holidays get under way.

"Give my love to Bess," I called as their car reversed and swung the corner out of sight.

I am writing this on the wooden kitchen table by lamplight while Léon prepares another fresh fish supper – he is quite a whizz in the kitchen. Father is reading the newspapers the Lautrecs brought with them for him. He has a thick brown envelope at his side. I don't know what is in it. I saw Claudette's father give it to him before they left. Money? False identity papers? Medical work of some sort?

Marek's birthday. Another year has passed…

30 July 1943

I noticed Father before he went to bed last night, checking the brown envelope. He has secreted it in the leather suitcase he received at Christmas. He checks it every night as if he fears its disappearance. I wonder if he might be saving funds in case of a sudden departure. Please, please not.

6 August 1943

Ghastly news from the coast, from Mérivel. Henri, the plumber's son from the village near Mérivel, who left with Robert to join the Résistance, has been murdered. We don't have too many details except that he was on a night-patrol task somewhere in the vicinity of Marseille and came up against a German troop, who arrested him along with several of his compatriots. They put him up against a firing squad at dawn the following morning, without a trial, and shot him in the head. There is no news of Robert. The Lautrecs have delayed their sojourn here with us to do what they can for Henri's family.

I hope I see Claudette again soon.

7 August 1943

More ghastly news. One of Hitler's top aides, a man called Heinrich Himmler, ordered the extermination of the ghettoes in Warsaw. I cannot say when his orders were given or carried out or what precisely has taken place. It was related to us by another family of Polish refugees here in Saint-Martin-Vésubie. It is impossible to know how accurate these snippets of information are. I cannot believe anybody would exterminate a whole inhabited zone. It sounds too criminal, too exaggerated.

8 September 1943

The Germans have arrived in Nice and they are hunting out Jews and making dozens of arrests.

It looks as though we will be leaving, Father, Léon and I. Yesterday, *Tata* and I did a very dangerous thing. We begged a lift from a local *commerce* man and returned to the coast to Mérivel, to say goodbye to our friends. While we were having a very quick lunch with them, *Tata* and I visited the estate chapel. There, we stood at mother's graveside for the last time. Father was crying. He was very silent about it, trying so very hard not to let me see his pain. When it was time, he took my hand and led me back to the bus station where we had arranged to meet Rémy, the butcher who had driven us down in his van. The streets of Nice were clogged with black Citroen cars. These were police, aiding the Germans on the lookout for *les Juifs*. Rémy's van reeked of dried blood. He had been delivering meat, lamb slaughtered yesterday in the mountains. Suddenly, I remembered our escape from Warsaw, all those years ago. What an odyssey we have travelled and there seems no end to it yet, but is there anywhere left for us to go? We have nowhere left to run to.

9 September 1943

"Pack only what is essential and wear sturdy shoes. Bring your coat as well. It will get cold. We have a lot of walking to do and we may be sleeping in places that are not heated."

"But it's still summer," I protested.

"Please don't argue, Rebecca robin."

"But where are we going?" I begged. "There is barely any place left in France for us to hide."

"We will cross the mountains into Italy. We'll be safe there."

"Why?"

"The Italians have surrendered," Léon reminded me, tugging at my cardigan to get me going. "They are supporting the Allies now."

"But everybody said that we were safe here…"

"Rebecca, get ready, please," Father insisted.

Léon offered to check over with me what I had packed to be sure that I had all I needed. I flared up. "I am not a child," I snapped. But I was not angry with him or Father, just angry that we are moving again. And I am frightened. Really frightened.

The Italians have moved out. The main body of soldiers have already left and returned to Italy. Only a small platoon is still in occupation and they can no longer protect us. Their concerns are with themselves now and their own safety.

10 September 1943

This morning we amassed in the central square, flocks of us: women, children, old and young people. All of us Jews. There must have been close to one thousand of us. All on the run, fleeing the imminent arrival of the Nazis.

There was an air of chaos about the town. A real sense of shock and panic. Many people had far too much baggage; others were crying; some, predominantly the elderly who had little ability to cross the mountains, were refusing to budge. I saw amongst them the woman who had travelled up with us on the bus all those months earlier. She looked very unwell. Those objecting said they would sit it out and that the centre for Jewish affairs in Nice would protect them.

Our last journey from Saint-Martin-Vésubie, our flight, led us first along a mule track that ran by a stream, eventually leading us to the Col de Fenestre. We passed by abandoned army barracks that had until days before been inhabited by Italians and then we made a tiring descent of almost 1,500 metres, trekking through quaint little villages, hamlets really, with Italian names although we were still on the French side of the border. I could hear water falling everywhere. Fast-flowing streams, waterfalls, rivers cascading downwards, amplified by the mountains. People trekked as fast or as slowly as they were able. Some moved with desperate purpose while others preferred to saunter. Mr Levitt and his family were right behind us. He was encouraging his children to sing, to do scales, attempting to keep their minds occupied.

"Rivka, sing us the first Hungarian folk song that comes into your head," he called to me. Before I could open my mouth, his eldest boy, young Franz, began a few melodic notes that were caught by his sister and others further back. I did not recognize the tune at all but it was lively and seemed to keep people's spirits up.

We lost sight of the Levitts when the younger son, Jacob,

needed to stop. His mother led both boys off the path and told them to pee behind a tree. His sister and father hung back waiting with them. "See you later in Cuneo, or on the boat to Palestine," Mr Levitt called out to us, jovially, full of optimism.

Léon was like a monkey the way he scooted on ahead, always determined to be sure that the way was clear for us, that the track had not been blocked, that no fallen tree or enemy barred our access. Father and I took it a little more steadily, conserving our energy. The three of us, along with a party of others from Saint-Martin, crossed over into Italy by way of the Valle Gesso. Once on the Italian side of the Alps, in Piedmont, fellow travellers thought they were safe and quite a large number took rooms for the night in a pretty little village called Entracque very close to the border, but we did not. We had planned to sleep rough, eat what we had brought with us or what Léon could hunt for us out in the wild. Father had said that we must conserve the finances we had (yes, the brown envelope!) until we reached Cuneo, about twenty kilometres further into Italy, where we were intending to take rooms and perhaps find some menial work for the winter. Léon picked us figs – our first Italian figs! – from a big old tree in Entracque. He swapped half a dozen of them for cheese from a woman at the roadside who waved to us and wished us well as she grinned toothlessly.

It was about then that we lost sight of the Levitt family, who had caught us up and then fallen behind again. What became of them? Father asked me. "Did you catch sight of them?" I assured him that we'd see them somewhere along the road, but we haven't crossed paths with them yet.

12 September 1943

What we had not calculated or even thought of was that the Germans might hit these border zones before us. Hitler has rescued or reinstated Mussolini, Italy's leader, and suddenly the Italians seem to be back fighting with Germany. It is all a state of confusion, tragic, inaccurate information. News is not reaching us way up here in this silent world of pine trees and mountain beasts. We are keeping ourselves off the beaten track, away from every living creature, but there are nights when we are awoken by noises, scufflings and cries, and the pounding of unseen hooves or feet on the ground. I thought they were wild animals but Léon seems less convinced. "It could be Germans," is his opinion.

13 September 1943

Keep moving, that is our decision, or rather *Tata* and Léon's. Many of the others who set off from Saint-Martin-Vésubie when we did have found places to stay. We are on our own now.

14 September 1943

We bought cheese from a shepherd. An Italian. He was young, toothless, a bit simple, but he recounted horrifying news. We are surrounded by Germans. They are looping the mountain ranges and dropping into villages, trapping and arresting, shooting some who were part of the largest of the parties who left Vésubie about the same time as us.

Can this be true or is he fancifying?

16 September 1943

We have reached the outskirts of Cuneo. The biggest shock is that the Germans are here ahead of us. Many of the surrounding villages have already been invaded. There was no chance for the Jews who had found refuge in any of these settlements.

An exhausted, disheartened body of about seventy travellers still shuffling onwards were easy prey for waiting soldiers who encircled them on a track on the outskirts of Cuneo. Hundreds of Jews have been captured and imprisoned in Cuneo, awaiting transportation. These are the snippets of stories that are being repeated to us.

We are retreating to a high forest area where we'll hide ourselves to keep out of danger. But the temperature is much lower and sleeping out at night is becoming more and more difficult. Also, we have no food. We are having to hunt for it or collect wild mushrooms. We have not resorted to stealing. Yet. How long we can survive in this fashion it's impossible to say. We are completely exhausted.

22 September 1943

What has saved us while others perished? Léon. He goes on ahead to scout and returns to report back to Father and to warn us when we must get off the road, or hang back out of sight and wait. Now, we are waiting.

We have set up camp by a river. So high are we that we are almost at its source. But I cannot calculate our exact position or even which side of the border we are travelling because we zigzag back and forth, and the frontier boundary is not straight, but I think we have been at this base for four days and nights now. Tiredness and hunger cloud my thinking process. We cannot light fires because it is not safe; we eat whatever prey can be trapped but we eat it raw. It is disgusting. A rabbit one day, a fish another. Or we fast.

The day before yesterday, a mongrel dog found us and slept with us, enjoying our company. Where he had come from, we couldn't say. A hunter's dog, a stray? He was a lovely, muscular little white thing with a black spot round his eye and two black front paws. Naturally, we nicknamed him Patch, which he seemed happy enough to answer to. He trailed along after us while we hunted for food throughout one morning, yapping at my ankles, but then, because we had nothing to offer him, he gave up and headed back to wherever he belonged. I was sorry when he left us. He had felt like a new friend.

24 September 1943

We are high above the outskirts of Cuneo, but we dare not enter the town. We are going to rethink our journey, our plans. I am writing this from a barn where we have hidden ourselves. There is one farm here but we haven't yet made ourselves known to the farmer. Will he turn us over to the Germans, as we have heard some peasants are doing, or will he and his family show us kindness, and offer us a hot meal or even a loaf of bread? Along the rocky pathway that led us here, we talked with another shepherd, who gave us milk. He confirmed that the Germans are in Cuneo. They have rounded up every Jew they could lay their hands on and shoved them into trains, into cattle trucks.

After all that time in France, surviving, keeping safe, so many of our own kind, refugees from eastern Europe, have not escaped.

We cannot survive out here alone with no resources and winter approaching. We have to make another plan or we will starve or be captured.

26 September 1943

This will be my last entry. I cannot write any more.

We are going to attempt to travel south, hugging the Mediterranean coast of Italy. Is this a wise decision? Wise or not, it appears to be our only option. If we turn back we will certainly meet the German armies. If we stay in this vicinity, we are likely to be captured or we will simply not find anywhere to rest for the winter and we will perish from hunger and cold. Our destination? Any port where we can find a boat. Some of our friends in Saint-Martin-Vésubie had their heart set on Palestine – they were calling that Mediterranean land, Eretz Israel – while others dreamed of the United States or South America. My father has talked of New York. But now that the time has come, if we can make our way safely and if we can find a passage, we will travel anywhere. Anywhere as long as it is away from here, away from everything we have experienced. In the end, all that matters now is to secure us a passage to somewhere. Somewhere far, far away from the war, from the fear for our lives, from the finger that points at us because we are who we are…

And so, my dearest Claudette, that is as far as my story goes. Or rather, the tales of my life in France. My diaries of those days, of you and Robert and Léon and Tata and my mother. To this day I do not know what happened to Mr Levitt and his family, my very inspiring piano teacher and the only man to beat my father at chess.

It was some time later that we learned the fate of those Jews who had remained behind in Saint-Martin-Vésubie. They were arrested, every one of them, by the German soldiers when they reached the village that had been our perfect idyll for so many months. It happened about twelve days after our departure. It seems quite possible that one or two local informers betrayed those who had stayed on. Horrible. I hope it was not anyone I had dealings with when we were living there. All were marched into buses, taken to the coast again, rounded up at the Hotel Excelsior in Nice and then herded out on trains to unspecified destinations. It was to Poland they were sent. They were not going home; they were headed to a place we knew nothing about back then, but have read a great deal about since. Auschwitz.

We were the lucky ones. We got out and we have survived. It took Father, Léon and me another two years and several false starts to board a boat for the United

States, but eventually in 1946, after the war had ended, our luck changed.

Léon is still with us. He travelled the entire distance in our company and was a great ally. Throughout all our months and then years of waiting to find a passage to New York, he and Father worked together, looking after the refugees we encountered along the way. Without medical equipment, the pair of them did what they could to heal and to comfort. Léon is studying medicine now here in New York City. He is training with Uncle Adam, who is a very famous psychiatrist, while Aunt Lidia continues to give her music lessons and, occasionally, public concerts. They have a very grand apartment on Park Avenue, which as you probably know is a very swish neighbourhood. Léon wants to work with patients who have been emotionally damaged by their experiences throughout the war. I think it is the perfect vocation for him.

And what of Aunt Irina and Marek? Marek, who is twelve years old now. We are not yet reunited with them but a few months ago we received a letter to say that both their names were on the passenger list of a boat that docked in Galveston, Texas in 1945. In fact, their liner arrived into America before we did. Now that we are settled, at some point very soon, we are intending to bring them here to live with us. However, there is bureaucracy and paperwork and it is not so simple. Aunt

Irina has married a Polish man she met during their passage from Lithuania and they have set up home in Texas. She and her husband are in the process of officially adopting Marek. They had heard nothing from us and had assumed that we had not survived and judged it the best solution for Marek. You see, everybody's story is complicated. But some of us have stories with happy endings and ours, thankfully, is one of them.

Please come and visit us. I will take you to all the best movie houses in New York and you will see what a handsome young doctor Léon is growing into. Are you training to be an actress? I am longing to hear from you about the Cannes Film Festival. Why was it not held this year? I went to see Brief Encounter, *the film that won the award the year before last. How I wept and thought of you. Oh, there is so much I want to gossip with you about. Please, please come to New York very soon and we can go dancing together and party. I remember well how you love to dance.*

By the way, I forgot to tell what I am doing with my life. I am at university and studying to be a journalist. I think after all that I have seen and the stories I have heard, it will be an exciting profession for me.

My dearest friend, I miss you so much.

Heaps of love,

Becky xx

Historical note

In 1930 the financial Depression that had crippled America reached Europe. Germany, still recovering from its humiliating defeat in the First World War, suffered greatly from this crisis. The country was already bankrupt and millions were unemployed. Discontent was mounting and it was fuelled by the National Socialists. An Austrian-born politician, Adolf Hitler, promised the dispirited German people that he would rid their nation of Jews and communists who, he claimed, were bleeding society. He also promised to reunite the German-speaking areas of Europe.

In July 1932 the National Socialist German Workers Party, known as the Nazi party, which Adolf Hitler had joined in 1920, received close to 40 per cent of the vote and became the strongest party in Germany.

On January 30 1933 President Paul von Hindenburg, under pressure, appointed Hitler Chancellor of Germany. Once in this position, Hitler moved swiftly and single-mindedly towards creating his dictatorship. He was on a dedicated mission. His goal was to restore glory to Germany and to bring about the perfect race.

Adolf Hitler's vendetta against the Jews was now accelerated. Anti-Semitic rhetoric had helped the Nazis win the election; now they were in a position to put some of their ideas into action.

In April 1933 Jews were banned from government jobs, a quota was established excluding Jews from university and a boycott of Jewish shops was enacted. When von Hindenburg died in August 1934, few paid attention. Hitler already had control of Germany...

The Nuremberg Laws were passed in 1935. These classed Jews as German "subjects" instead of citizens. Intermarriage was outlawed, more professions were closed to Jews, shops displayed signs reading, "No Jews Allowed". Harassment became a common theme.

In October 1938 another attempt to purge Germany of its Jews took place with a round-up of those holding Polish citizenship. These Polish Jews were transported to the Polish border and abandoned. There, the Polish authorities kept them in a no-man's land.

One of the deported Polish Jewish families wrote to their seventeen-year-old son, Herschel Grynszpan, who was studying in Paris, recounting all that had taken place.

When Grynszpan read of the torments his parents had suffered, he resolved to avenge them. At the German Embassy in Paris, he shot dead a German diplomat, vom Rath. This act of revenge against a German citizen was the perfect opportunity for Hitler. The Nazis called for demonstrations and reprisals. Violence erupted everywhere across the Third Reich and continued for two days. Stores were destroyed, synagogues burned, and 20,000 Jews arrested. The riots became known as Kristallnacht – the Night of Glass – for all the broken glass.

The "Jewish Problem" obsessed Adolph Hitler and he was determined within his Nazi Germany, the Third Reich, to resolve it, to rid Germany of all Jews. In 1939, he published a citizen's handbook. It was intended to provide the Third Reich with a guide to the handling of the "Jewish Problem".

From 1933 onwards Jews across northern Europe had been growing very concerned. Hitler's expansionist policy meant that Jews beyond German borders were also at risk. Many Jewish families and individuals, including esteemed writers, journalists and artists, began to flee to safer territories. Until late 1939 France was deemed to be a safe alternative.

On 16 March 1939 Hitler invaded Czechoslovakia and took control of the entire country. Jews still living there were at grave risk. Many were arrested. On 1 September Hitler invaded Poland. On 3 September Britain, followed several hours later by France, declared war on Germany.

At this stage, Jewish citizens from across eastern and northern Europe were still arriving into France believing it to be a safe zone.

On 10 May 1940 German air raids attacked Belgium

and Holland. The Germans fought their way through Luxembourg and Belgium. Their goal was France. The attacks came from France's northern border, in a surprise incursion. The French were not prepared because they had set up their defence line further south. Northern France fought hard, but the German armies were swift and merciless.

On 3 June the first German bombs fell on Paris. Citizens begin to flee, heading south where they believed they would be out of reach of the war and the invading forces. This mass exodus of people included ordinary French citizens as well as Jews. It caused chaos on the roads and in the south. Southern France was not at all prepared for the millions of extra people looking for homes and food.

The French Government, fearing for its safety, quit the capital and fled to Bordeaux on 13 June. And on 14 June Paris fell to the Germans. Tanks rolled into the capital. and the swastika flag was flown throughout the city.

His nation beaten and demoralized, the Prime Minister of France, Paul Renaud, resigned on 16 June. Marshal Philippe Pétain, a World War I French war hero, formed a new government.

France surrendered to Germany on 22 June. Revelling in his victory, Hitler insisted on signing the document of capitulation in the same railway carriage that had been used when Germany surrendered to France in 1918. For France, this was perceived as the ultimate humiliation.

The world was shocked that one of its strongest nations could have been overcome in a matter of weeks. It would be left to the British and her allies along with support from the United States to stand up to Hitler. But the US support took time.

Under the terms of the armistice, France was divided into two sections: the north was ruled by Germany and the south, the Free Zone, was governed from the spa town of Vichy under the leadership of Marshal Pétain. Unfortunately, even this supposedly independent French government was found to be collaborating with the Germans. Amongst government acts, later judged as treason, was the removal of many Jews from France to undeclared destinations in northern Europe over the next four years. The transported Jews were both French nationals and foreign refugees who had fled from other parts of Europe seeking exile in France.

One of the few glimmers of hope for France's liberation came from the energy and vision of another French military figure, a soldier who exiled himself in London rather than surrender to the Germans, General Charles de Gaulle. Soon after France's surrender, de Gaulle broadcast a radio message from London confirming that there were French who would fight on.

Over the next four years, resistance groups burgeoned throughout France, fast becoming a strong fighting force, but they always worked as secret operations and in hiding. If their operations became known, they risked reprisals being brought against the country's civilian population and the punishments proved to be very harsh.

General de Gaulle continued his campaign from his home of exile in London. His broadcasts to the citizens of France during the war years have become famous.

The Americans, led by their President Franklin Roosevelt, joined the war in 1941. The Allies were gaining ground in North Africa and then southern Italy. The Germans feared that France would be entered from the south and liberated. If Hitler intended to keep France, he decided that he needed to control all of France.

On 11 November 1942 German forces invaded the unoccupied zone of Southern France. One of the repercussions of this was that Jews who had found a degree of safety in Southern France were once more in danger. Yet again, they found themselves on the run. Worse, the Vichy government was actively aiding Germany in the round-up of Jews.

However, due to an unlikely set of circumstances, one tiny pocket of France remained safe for Jews. This was in the hinterland villages behind the Riviera city of Nice. The reason Jews found a haven there was because, for a short while, this area of France was policed by the Italians, who were Hitler's allies. However, Italy had no desire to persecute the Jews and disregarded Hitler's order to arrest them and put them in freight trains for transportation to eastern Europe.

In 1943 the Allies invaded Italy and eventually Italy surrendered. All Italian troops were pulled out of Southern France. This left the Jewish refugees in a very precarious situation. There was nowhere left for them to run to. Many tried to escape across the Alps but were either killed in the effort or captured by the Nazis who had, by this time, crossed France and were entering Italy. Thousands and thousands of Jewish refugees who had managed to survive the war thus far were now put on trains and sent to undeclared locations. Later, it was discovered that their destinations were concentration camps where they were exterminated. The most renowned of these camps was in Poland, Auschwitz.

In 1945 France was liberated, the Nazis surrendered and Hitler committed suicide in a bunker in Berlin.

Approximately 11 million people were murdered as a result of Hitler's genocidal policy. These included Jews, Gypsies, communists, homosexuals and some who were disabled. Hitler's Nazi regime was responsible for the deaths of more than six million Jews. This programme of the systematic annihilation of Jewish people became known as the Holocaust or in Hebrew, *Shoah*.

Of the nine million Jews residing in Europe before the war, it is estimated that two-thirds perished. It is generally held that the ordinary German people, those who were not members of Hitler's special armies and bureaucracy, were unaware of the atrocities taking place, particularly

Turn the page for an extract from
My Story: The Hunger,
also by Carol Drinkwater

May 10 1845

Ah, Lord, isn't this great! A book full of empty pages and all of them for me. Today is my fourteenth birthday and my big brother Patrick gave me this to write in. "A way to keep hold of your thoughts, Phylly," he said. "To store up your secrets and dreams and build them into a world where you can roam freely wherever and whenever it takes your fancy."

Where to start? Oh, my name! Should I introduce myself to myself? Well, I will. Out of politeness and to give the pages a beginning. My name is Phyllis McCormack and those who love me, which is my family, call me Phylly. I live in Queen's County in the south of Ireland. We are Irish Catholics, and I can read and wri—

There's Ma calling! This is Phylly McCormack signing off. I have just realized that I haven't told a thing about myself or my life. Coming Ma! I'll begin with that tomorrow then.

May 11 1845

It's me again! I love this! I've been going about my day, helping with chores, my mind racing with the things I want to set down in my own private book!

Here's how we live. There's Ma and Da, then there's Pat, the eldest boy, and after him, me. Then, in age order, there's Hughie who's ten, Grace who is eight, Mikey's four and, lastly, baby Eileen who's six months. It's a struggle for space. We've just the one room and a covered bit out back where Ma and Da sleep. Still, we are blessed at our cottage because we have a bed, although we don't have covers for it. I have never visited one of those households where they have bedclothing. Irish linen and that kind of fancy stuff is produced up north and then shipped to England or France. Usually, it's bought by rich landowners. Most families here sleep on straw but, as I said, we have a bed.

What else? Oh, yes, we own a very greedy pig and a piglet. We feed them coarse potatoes – they're lumpier than the ones we grow for our own consuming. In the summer, when the pig has got nice and fat, Da takes it to market and sells it for cash. This money pays towards our rent. Da keeps a little in reserve to make sure we can buy food, if we need to. For, by summer, our potato stock has run low and we have little to eat. Our lives are about scratching a living off the land.

My parents farm 16 acres, all of it rented. There are many who survive on less than five but those poor families are always close to starving, whatever season it is.

We are one of the few families in the neighbourhood who have a dog. He's called Mutt. He's black and wiry and a real mix of a fellow. I found him a year back running wild on the road, wounded, starving-thin and I begged Da to let me keep him. Da said yes, on condition that not one morsel of our food was spent on him and that, should things get bad again – meaning if there was another famine like the one in 1822, way before I was born – then I'd put him back out on the road to fend for himself. I agreed, but I never would. Next to Pat, I love Mutt best in all the world.

We also have a couple of chickens, which is another luxury. So, we are not so poor. In fact, we are better off than almost every family within walking distance of our crossroads. Our cottage is not insulated against the weather but we burn bog peat in the winter, which keeps us warm as toast. It gets awful smoky though because we don't have a chimney but, all in all, we are a happy band, us McCormacks. I have nothing to complain of. Except that I wish I was a boy!

May 12 1845

How is it that I can read and write and dozens of others, including Ma and Da, cannot? Well, in 1829, Daniel O'Connell – he's our national hero and I'll write more about him later – won back equal rights for Catholics. So now, we are entitled to go to school. I go to school and Pat went to school.

Pat says the pen is the purest weapon in the world. Da says Pat is a dreamer and nothing comes of dreams. But I'd follow him to the end of the world. Pat's dreaming makes the world shiny and bright. At school, I learn English and spelling. Mathematics too, but I'm not great with sums. Sometimes, if we are lucky, we learn geography. I love that best. I am always daydreaming about faraway places. I stare at the maps and picture myself travelling the whole world wide. I can point out France and England and the New World of America, which is bigger than both of the others stitched together. One day, I want to sail to America on one of those grand steamers I've seen in drawings. I shan't be afraid, even though I've never seen the sea.

There is another place on the map, big as America, but it's terrible far away. When we speak of it, it is with dread or sadness. It is a huge continent of a place called Australia and next to it is a smaller landmass, Van Diemen's Land. I don't ever want to go to those places for they are where the convicts are sent on the transportation ships.

May 13 1845

Ah, but this is grand! Having a diary of my own is like having a best friend who will never give my secrets away. But will I ever have any secrets that are *so* secret you grow breathless when you think them? This morning, when Pat and I were scything the grass, I asked him what sort of secrets he thought I should be filling these pages with. He threw back his head and laughed so loud I thought he'd crack open the blue sky overhead.

"You'll know them, Phylly, when you start thinking and feeling them. Trust me."

"So how should I fill the blank pages until they do occur to me?" I asked him.

"Write about yourself, and write about Ireland. Ireland as you see her and live her. Tell it through your eyes, Phylly."

"That's family and school and history," I said to Pat. "My diary will be boring then, because I'm no *seanchaí*!" *Seanchaí* is the Irish word for storyteller.

"Who knows, one day, you might be a real storyteller, little sister. Yes, I can see you as the red-haired, freckled *seanchaí* who travels the New World recounting tales of Ireland."

Later, I was thinking over what Pat had said and it seemed such a grand notion, to write about Ireland and travel the world with my tales. It would be the best dream in the world but I have no idea how I could ever achieve such a thing. What chance have I, an Irish country girl, of ever sailing the seas and visiting the New World of America? But I can begin with everything I see around me now. I shall write of what makes me happy and what makes me sad or afraid.